MW01017369

The Last Story, the First Story

THE LAST STORY, THE FIRST STORY

by Richard Thompson

Annick Press Ltd.
Toronto, Canada

Cover art by David Simpson

Annick Press gratefully acknowledges the
contributions of The Canada Council and
the Ontario Arts Council

Canadian Cataloguing in Publication Data

Thompson, Richard, 1951–
    The last story, the first story

(Annick young novels)
ISBN 1-55037-025-1 (bound). – ISBN 1-55037-024-3 (pbk.)

I. Ohi, Ruth. II. Title.
III. Series.

PS8589.H65L37 1988   jC813′.54   C88-094085-9
PZ7.T46La 1988

Distributed in Canada and the USA by:
Firefly Books Ltd.
3520 Pharmacy Ave. Unit 1c
Scarborough, Ontario
M1W 2T8

Printed and bound in Canada
by Gagné Printing Ltd.

For Michael Glover

Contents

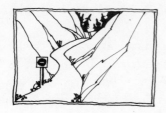

CHAPTER ONE... in which Summer and her Dad finally get the van going but Summer doesn't make it to the horse show after all

"I can't see anything coming!" Summer hollers.

The van starts to roll slowly backwards, the tires scrunching in the gravel.

"Okay," Larry yells, *"start turning the wheel!"*

Summer starts pulling the steering wheel slowly to the left as Larry had shown her. She can feel the front of the van begin to swing. She can see Larry's head through the windshield as he leans his weight against the front of the van. The top of his bald head has gone bright red with the effort of pushing.

"More!"

Summer pulls the wheel harder. She glances over her shoulder back along the narrow road toward the crest of the hill. Any minute something is bound to come barrelling along over that hill...

"Hurry up, Larry!" she thinks. *"Push harder!"*

"Pull on the brake!" Larry calls. Summer reaches down and pulls up on the emergency brake handle. Larry comes around to the door, mopping the top of his head and grinning. "Alright," he says. "Halfway there. Okay now, Summer, you slide over and hold the wheel straight while I push. When we're rolling, I'll jump in. Okay, let off the brake."

Summer releases the brake lever and very slowly the van starts to move. Little by little, it picks up speed. Larry grabs the steering wheel and jumps up into the seat, slamming the door behind him.

The van continues to pick up speed.

"Here goes nothing," says Larry. He pushes in the clutch pedal. The engine moans, coughs...

"Come on! Come on!"

...and roars to life.

"Alright! Excellent!" Larry hollers. He reaches over and shakes Summer by the shoulder. "We're in business, daughter!" he laughs. Then he bounces a couple of times and settles in the seat. "Just have to remember that, if we're going to stop, we gotta stop on a hill!"

A few minutes later, the battered old van is shuddering along the gravel road.

"I'll tell you what, Summer," says Larry. "I'm going to drop you at the Exhibition Grounds. You can go find Lynn and go to the horse show together, and then..."

"We won't make it, Larry," says Summer.

"After the horse show, I'll pick you both up, and we can go to the Triple Star for Chinese food. Don't worry; we've got lots of time."

"You always say that," protests Summer, "and half the time we never get there!"

"And half the time we do," says Larry amiably. "That's not a bad average, eh? Fifty-fifty. Relax."

"How am I supposed to relax, Larry! I promised Lynn that I'd be there. She'll be disappointed if I miss her first show."

"She'll understand if we are a bit late. We're not going to be late, but if we are..."

"We will be."

"If we are, she'll understand that it wasn't your fault."

"I hate this stupid van," says Summer. "Every time we need it, it breaks down!"

Larry turns his head toward her. He looks like a giant elf with his Granny glasses perched on his round nose. He grins.

"Nobody can stay mad when they're eating egg rolls at the Triple Star." Larry winks at her.

Sometimes it seems like her father never takes anything seriously.

"Don't worry..."

Suddenly, the grin vanishes, Larry's body tenses, his head moves forward. Summer's eyes follow his, and her heart clenches in her chest.

A logging truck is coming straight toward them!

Larry cranks the steering wheel hard, and the van lurches crazily to the right.

Even as she throws up her hands, Summer thinks, "There aren't supposed to be any logging trucks on the road on Saturdays!"

The windshield goes milky white, and the

crumbles of glass are spraying into the air like globs
of icy rain. Summer clamps her eyes shut tight. She
feels herself lifting, flying.

* * *

"Summer!"

The pictures stopped. Her mother was calling her from up at the house.

"Down at the creek, Mom!" Summer hollered back.

"Come up!" The house was half a kilometre away and at the top of a high bluff, but her mother's voice carried clearly on the shimmering July air. "I've got a surprise for you."

"I'll be right there."

Summer looked at the curious object that she was holding in her hands. She had found it tangled in the roots of the old spruce that had fallen in the big wind storm that spring. Ralph had led her to the spot. The dog had taken off after something, barking furiously, and Summer had followed him to the fallen tree. Whatever it was had gotten away, or Ralph had simply lost interest, but there amongst the snake-twisting roots of the tree, Summer had found the thong. It was made of dry, cracked leather which had been knotted and pieced into a strand. An odd collection of things were threaded onto it or attached to it with loops of leather cord—small bones, pieces of carved wood, feathers, small polished stones, shells, shapes made of clay, shards of metal.

"Why did the pictures start when I picked this up?" thought Summer, as she started to wind the thong into a loose coil. "Why those pictures?"

Always—for as long as she could remember remembering—she'd seen pictures in her head.

"Summer, stop daydreaming!" her teachers would scold.

But it wasn't like dreaming, exactly. It was more like... like watching a movie. Larry had seemed to understand. He'd laughed when she'd talked to him about it once, but it was the laugh he laughed that said, "Right on! Excellent, man!"

Karen was waiting for her on the deck when Summer got to the top of the path. She was grinning from ear to ear.

"Guess who's in the house?" she said.

Larry's face popped into Summer's mind, and instantly faded again.

"I don't know," she said.

"Come on! Guess!" insisted her mom.

Her mother loved to make you play guessing games, and if you couldn't guess, she'd give you clues all afternoon until you did. Mercifully, the visitor gave the game away.

A tall, blond boy stepped out onto the porch. He held out his arms dramatically, acknowledging an imaginary adoring crowd.

"Tah! Tah!"

"Orin!" cried Summer.

She tossed the thong onto one of the rickety chairs on the porch and threw her arms around her mother. "Mom!" she laughed. "Orin's here!"

He looked the same, right down to the cassette player clipped to the waistband of his pants. He was a bit taller maybe, and his hair was shorter...

15

"Glad to see me?" said the boy. "Ecstatic, in fact?"

Ralph, Summer's big yellow dog, waddled around the corner of the house and stood beside Orin grinning a doggy grin and thumping his tail against his leg.

"Ralph, at least, is ecstatic."

"I'm mildly ecstatic," said Karen. "Not as ecstatic as Ralph, but . . ."

"I'm ecstatic, too!" laughed Summer.

Summer often thought of Orin as her best friend, and just as often thought that he was a strange best friend for a girl like her to have. Both her family and Orin's had chosen to leave the city to pursue the dream of a life of independence, living with and off the land. Summer couldn't remember any other kind of life, and even if she sometimes resented the isolation, the hard work and the lack of the little luxuries—TV for instance—she knew she fit there.

Orin, on the other hand, never did seem to fit into his family's dream. He wasn't comfortable around animals or growling chainsaws. He didn't like outdoor toilets, or cold floors in the morning. He missed TV, and he missed having ten kids to play with just down the block.

"I would have adapted in time," he told Summer. "I'm very adaptable."

Summer wasn't so sure that Orin would ever have become a country boy, but, as it turned out, he'd never had a chance to find out. The dream, it seemed, had been not the family's dream but Orin's father's dream. And his mother hadn't adapted.

Within two years, she had left for Vancouver taking Orin and his sister Aleisha with her. That was three years ago. The two children came now to stay with their father only during the summer holidays.

"Where's Aleisha?" asked Summer.

"She said to tell you she will come over tomorrow. She was too sleepy after the night on the bus."

"Come on in the house," said Summer's mother. "You've got a lot of catching up to do."

And so the long, warm afternoon was spent in talk and talk and more talk.

"It's sure super to see you guys again!" said Orin. Summer was washing the supper dishes; he was drying. "The city is great, but I miss being here with Dad and with you and Karen and..."

The kitchen was suddenly very quiet.

The counter, the dishpan full of suds, her reflection in the window—all became a blur as tears clouded Summer's eyes. And then all she could see was the pictures...

* * *

His glasses are lying in the gravel, one lens cracked neatly across the middle.

"Larry will need his glasses," she thinks. "He can't see a thing without his glasses..."

But when she reaches out to pick them up, pain screeches along her arm. There is blood on her hand, and she doesn't know why. She tries to bring her hand to her nose to see if it's bleeding; she gets nose bleeds sometimes if it's really hot. The pain screams at her as soon as she tries to move.

She struggles to her knees. Why is she on the ground?

Then she sees the logging truck. It's parked at a crazy angle, one front wheel cocked up on the bank. A man in a baseball cap is hanging onto the open door, talking into the handset of a CB radio.

And then she remembers! She lurches to her feet, oblivious of the pain.

"Larry!" she screams. "Larry!"

She can't see him. The van is on its side in the ditch, the front crumpled like tin foil, one wheel wrenched completely off. But she can't see her father.

She tries to run toward the van.

"No, don't go over there, kid! Please, don't."

The man in the baseball cap is holding her arms, so she can't run. Summer twists out of his grip, but he grabs her again. She turns and kicks out at him.

"Let me go!" she screams, and he does.

She runs toward the van.

*   *   *

Crash! A plate slipped from Summer's hands and smashed on the kitchen floor.

Summer shook the suds off her hands, and without a word, turned and walked out.

The workshop was about a hundred metres from the house nestled among the pine trees on the far side of the chicken coop.

Summer went in and closed the door behind her. She stood in the dusty, oil-smelling twilight, sobbing quietly. After a while, she sniffed and wiped her tears on the sleeve of her sweat shirt. Taking a flashlight from a shelf by the door, she crouched down and pulled a wooden box out from under the work bench.

She let the beam of the flashlight play over the collection of objects in the box—a pair of wire-rimmed glasses with one lens cracked neatly across the middle, a Swiss Army knife, a plastic pouch with a picture of a sailboat on it, a file, a screwdriver, several worn cleats from a cork boot, a piece of harness strap, a chess man, photographs, a book, three empty shell casings, a grey and white wool toque... Larry's things, all that she had left.

The noise was sharp and distinct, an intrusion in the warm twilight, an intrusion on her thoughts. She glanced up to see the silhouette of a boy peering at her through the glass. A quick intake of breath, a tightening in her stomach—the flashlight slipped out of her hand, and rolled away under the bench—and then the face was gone.

The jolt of fear gave way to a wave of anger. Summer sprang to her feet. "Orin!" she yelled. She raced to the door and pulled it open. "Orin Webb, don't go sneaking around spying on people!"

She stalked the whole way around the workshop, but Orin had managed to slip away. She looked behind the woodshed and the chicken coop, and then decided—"To heck with it!"—and went back to the house.

Orin and her mother were at the kitchen table with a photo album open in front of them—Summer's album. Summer recognized the photos—ones she'd taken of Larry and Ralph. She grabbed the album and slammed it shut.

"Orin Webb, you're a creep!" she said.

"Wha...?" Orin blinked at her.

"Don't act innocent! I saw you spying on me."

"Summer, is something bothering you?" asked her mother. "Calm down."

"I'm calm!" said Summer. "I just don't like people peering in windows at me..."

"What are you talking about?" said her mother. "Orin has been here with me since we finished the dishes."

Summer looked at the two of them sheepishly, and let her arms drop to her sides. Then she pulled out a chair and slumped onto it wearily. "Sorry," she said. "I'm sorry."

"That's okay," said Orin. "I don't mind being called a creep. That's Aleisha's favourite name for me." He laughed uneasily.

"Are you okay, Summer?" asked her mother.

"Yeah, I'm okay," Summer replied.

"Do you want to talk?"

How many times had Karen asked her that since the accident—a hundred, a thousand? Couldn't she understand that talking was a way of remembering; and all Summer wanted was to forget.

"No," said Summer. "No, I don't want to talk."

"...because if I do the pictures will start going in my head," she thought, "and I don't want to see those pictures again..."

"Hey, I better be going," said Orin. "I'll see you tomorrow, eh, Summer?"

"Yeah," said Summer. She glanced up, but didn't meet his eyes. "I'll see you tomorrow."

CHAPTER TWO...where Summer and Orin go to get water and discover a secret passage

"In the land of Oz..."

Knees, clap, cross right, clap, cross left...

"Where the ladies smoke cigars..."

The two girls sitting in the sun in the window seat kept the beat crossing left, clap, right, clap...

"Every breath they take is enough to kill a snake..."

"What do you think this weird thing is?"

The loud shout broke Summer's concentration, and she missed the beat. "Sorry, Aleisha," she said to her partner.

She scowled at Orin slouched in an armchair by the fireplace. His ears were covered by the foam ear pieces of the portable cassette player from which Summer could hear, even on the other side of the room, the faint clatter of a rock band. In his hands he held the strange thong that Summer had found a couple of days earlier.

"Did you say you found this out in the bush somewhere?" he shouted.

"I found it on that spruce tree down by the creek," Summer replied. "The one that blew down in the storm."

"What?"

Summer stood up, crossed the room and pulled off the earphones. "Orin Webb," she said, "if you want to talk to me, take that thing off. I'm not going to compete with the 'Cracked Bananas' or the 'Waddling Drakes' or whoever it is."

Orin prided himself on his esoteric musical tastes. Last year it had been obscure country and western bands like 'The Campfire Crooners', 'The Saddle Burrs' and 'The Snowy Drifters'. This year it was even more obscure rock groups like...

"'The Allergic Reactions'... a great group!" said Orin. "Sorry. I forgot I had the Walkman on."

"He's always forgetting," said Aleisha. "And sometimes he starts singing along. He sounds awful. Actually, he sounds awful even without the earphones on, but he sounds worse with them."

"From a person whose favourite vocalist is Cookie Monster, that's a compliment," said Orin. He walked across the room and tossed the cassette player onto the window seat beside his sister.

"Here," he said. "Listen to some 'Allergic Reactions' for a while. It'll broaden your horizons."

"But Summer and me..."

"*Summer and I* are busy solving the puzzle of this ancient artefact."

22

"I don't know if it's that ancient," said Summer. "That belt buckle is pretty modern."

"I think it might be something to do with the Carrier Indians who used to live around here," said Orin. He twined the thong around his neck several times.

"Caveman designer jewellery! What do you think!"

"I think you should borrow it," said Summer. "You'd be right in fashion when you go back to Vancouver."

"I think I *will* borrow it!" declared Orin. He paraded in front of the mirror, striking poses.

"Summer!"

Orin and Aleisha followed Summer into the studio at the front of the house where her mother was sitting at the bench stitching on one of the soft sculpture dolls that she sold at craft fairs in the valley.

"Can you go down to the pond and get a bucket of water, Summer, we're almost out," she said. She pulled on the needle and the mouth on the face in her hand puckered into a smile. "Thanks. The clean buckets are by the door."

"I'll come," said Orin.

"Well, if Orin is going with you," said Karen, "you might as well get two buckets."

"I'll go, too!" chimed in Aleisha.

"Oh, good!" said Orin. "You haven't met the ghost yet, have you? Now's your chance!"

"That's just a silly story, Orin, and you know it. There's no ghost in the pond. Is there, Karen?"

"Well, I've never actually seen anything, but

that's what people told us when we bought this place—that the pond was haunted by the ghost of a young girl. Larry said he saw her once."

Summer knocked over the pile of plastic buckets with a loud clatter. Karen glanced in her direction and went on with her story.

"She was there on the bottom with her hair floating around her head like seaweed. He said she seemed to be trying to speak to him, but, of course, he couldn't hear what she was trying to say."

"Well, are you coming or not?" asked Orin. Aleisha hesitated uneasily.

"Why don't you stay and help me pack up some of these dolls," said Karen, putting down her sewing and standing up purposefully.

"Okay," said Aleisha.

"And if you two do see the ghost, invite her to come up for supper." Karen winked at Summer as they headed out the door.

"My Walkman!" said Orin. "I need my Walkman!"

"I'll get it," Aleisha volunteered.

"Thank you, child," said Orin, taking the cassette player from his sister. "From time to time, you can be quite tolerable. —Wait up!"

He grabbed his bucket and headed out the door after Summer.

"We walked up the creek for miles last fall," said Summer, "and we found this spring where it starts. There was this big cliff, kind of, and the water was trickling out of all these little cracks. That's why the creek never dries up completely—because of the spring."

They came shortly to the spot where the path was blocked by the fallen trunk of a large spruce tree. Summer swung herself over the tree trunk and took the buckets from Orin. A few metres further along, the creek dribbled into a wide, still pond. An ancient tamarack had been uprooted and lay with its top tangled in the brown-green waters several metres from the edge of the pond. Its roots rested on the bank like a huge fist with its fingers wrapped around a gigantic handful of earth.

"Coming down is always the easy part!" said Orin. He put down his bucket and sat down on the lid.

"It *is* a bit of a nuisance having to come down to the creek for water," said Summer. "The old timers around here thought Mom and Dad were crazy building the house up on the hill when there wasn't any water there. But they liked the view."

"Crazy hippies!" growled Orin.

Summer laughed. "Yep, that's what you old-timers always said."

"Orin! Summer!" Aleisha was calling to them.

"Come on. We'd better get the water and get back," said Summer. "The best way is to go out on the tree and scoop it out of the deep part, so you don't get dirt in it."

"That wasn't there before, was it?" asked Orin, pointing to the fallen tamarack.

"That's one of the trees that blew down this

spring. Larry was going to build a platform so we could get out to the deep part of the pond..."

"I guess he doesn't have to now," said Orin. He blushed. "I mean this is just as good..."

"It's okay," said Summer. "I know what you meant." She scrambled up onto the scaly trunk of the tree.

"No, wait!" said Orin. "I'll do it!"

Summer shrugged. "Sure, if you like."

"Just let me take this off," said Orin as he unhooked his Walkman and hung it on one of the roots of the tamarack. "You can't be too careful."

"Well, if you're planning to fall in, you should take off my thong, too," suggested Summer.

Orin unwound the thong and handed it to Summer. Then, picking up a bucket, he climbed onto the tree trunk, got awkwardly to his feet and started to walk slowly and cautiously down toward the water. After a couple of tries, he managed to get the mouth of the bucket into the water and pulled it up about a quarter full. He stood up gingerly and started to pick his way back up the trunk.

"Orin," said Summer, "can't you get a bit more than that?"

"This is lots," muttered Orin.

"Here, I'll do it," said Summer. "I'm used to it." She hung the thong on the root next to the Walkman and climbed up onto the tree. She started down toward Orin.

"Go back!" Orin said. "There isn't room."

"Of course, there's room," said Summer. "Just

give me the bucket. And now just stand still and I'll go around you. There's lots of room."

"No! I'm going to fall!" Orin started to tip backwards. He clutched at Summer. Orin hollered and Summer yelled, and they both toppled off the tree, splashed into the pond and sank.

Summer felt water go up her nose and twisted to get upright. She felt a moment of panic as something grabbed at her. A high sweet voice sang in her ears—"Mother! Mother!"—and she imagined silver ghost fingers clutching at her. She tugged, and the branch that had snagged on her shirt snapped. She bobbed to the surface.

A moment later, Orin burst from below, sputtering and flailing his arms.

"Holy! I thought I was going to drown!" he gasped. "I could feel something grabbing at me ..."

Summer felt a cold shiver crawl down her body. "Come on," she said. "Let's get out of here. It's cold."

They paddled to the edge of the pond, squelched through the sodden ooze and flopped onto the bank.

"You really should consider a better system for getting water," said Orin, as he lay back on the grass. He looked at his watch, a hi-tech wonder in chrome and plastic. "Thank goodness, my watch is totally waterproof," he said. He pushed the buttons, checking just in case. "All functions functional," he said with satisfaction. "And I had the good sense to take off my Walkman before I went out on that log." He stood up and walked over to the tree.

"It's gone!"

"What?"

"My tape player. I put it on those roots, and now it's gone!"

"The thong is gone, too!" said Summer. "I left it with your Walkman."

"Aleisha!" said Orin. "This is the work of my pestiferous little sister."

"Look, Orin!" said Summer pointing. "Something is moving down there."

"Aleisha Webb, you are going to die!" yelled Orin, jumping up and sprinting along the path toward the meadow.

"Wait!" called Summer. "I don't think it's Aleisha!"

When she caught up with him, Orin was sitting on the trunk of the fallen spruce tree.

"She got away!" he muttered. "I saw her at the tree and the next second she was gone..."

A faint rattling noise came from behind the upturned base of the tree. Quickly, Summer scrambled up the bank, expecting to see Aleisha crouching behind the roots of the tree with an impish smile on her face. There was no one there.

Orin clambered up beside her. "Did you see her?"

"No," said Summer, "but I thought I heard something... Wait a minute! What's that?"

A large boulder protruded from the wall of the crater, and looking more closely, Summer realized that what had at first seemed to be its shadow was, in fact, a small opening.

"There's a tunnel or a cave under that rock," she said.

"Are you sure?" asked Orin, following behind.

"Yeah! Look!"

She was crouching down, looking at an opening maybe half a metre high and nearly as wide, just big enough for a person to crawl into.

"She wouldn't have gone in there..."

Orin knelt in the opening and called, "Aleisha!" His voice echoed in the hollow.

He crawled part way into the opening.

"Orin!" cried Summer. A sense of dread seemed to fill her chest, a breathless feeling. "You can't go in there. It might cave in."

"It's hard to see, but I think there's a pretty big cave..."

Orin edged a bit further into the opening and called his sister's name again.

"Orin," Summer pleaded, "don't be stupid! Come back!" His feet slithered through the opening, and he disappeared from sight.

"Hey! I can stand up!" he shouted. "This must be an old mine or something!"

"Orin!" Summer shouted, panic edging into her voice. "Come out!"

"I'm just going to go a bit farther."

"Orin, come back!" Summer said between clenched teeth. It was a kind of prayer.

"Summer!" Orin's voice boomed out through the opening. "I found the Walkman! She's got to be in here! Aleisha! Aleisha AAAAAAAAAA!"

The final sound of the name echoed on and on—and then there was silence.

"Orin? Orin, can you hear me? ORIN!"

CHAPTER THREE...where they can't find Aleisha, and Orin disappears in the cave

"I'm blind!" Orin gropes about in the darkness, screaming in panic. "I'm blind! I'm blind! Ow!" He puts out his hands and feels stone, a stone wall. The stone and the pain give a shape to the darkness; the panic subsides, and he can think. He's in a cave, and he's fallen.

"I must have knocked myself unconscious," he says to himself.

"Summer!" he calls. The sound echoes crazily around him for what seems like a long time. No one answers. "Summer!" Why doesn't she answer?

The silence flows in around him like thick, black syrup. Then, faintly, he can hear a voice, Aleisha's voice, calling, "Orin! Help me! Orin! Orin, I'm here!"

He gropes his way toward the voice, cursing as

he cracks his foot against a rock, bangs his arm against a jutting root.

He calls back. "Aleisha!"

"Orin! Help me!" The voice seems farther away.

"Stand still, Aleisha! Don't move! I'm coming!"

He falls and gets up again, scrambling along blindly.

* * *

Summer's foot twisted on a loose rock, and she went down hard on one knee.

"Ow!"

With the sudden pain, Orin in the cave vanished, and Summer was aware of herself again—aware of the ache in her legs, the sweat stinging in her eyes, the breath rasping in her throat. She grasped a small tree, pulled herself up and sprinted the last ten metres up the path to the house.

"Mom!"

The studio was empty. Summer ran into the kitchen.

"Mom!" Where was she? Summer climbed up the loft stairs just far enough to see through the railing that her mother wasn't there either.

And she wasn't feeding the chickens. The chickens blucked and strutted in their wire-wrapped yard, totally unconcerned about the knot of dread growing in the pit of Summer's stomach.

Her mother wasn't in the woodshed either, or in the outhouse. Where was she?

"Mom!" Summer called as loud as she could. She stood still and listened for the answer. A chainsaw snarled faintly, far away across the valley. A pine

32

cone skittered down from the top of a tree as a squirrel started along a branch.

"Where *is* she?" Summer yelled, and turned and sprinted back toward the house.

She looked in all the rooms she'd looked in before, knowing before she looked that her mother would not be there.

The note was lying on the kitchen table.

"Summer and Orin," it read in Karen's fat round handwriting. 'Aleisha and I have taken Ralph for a walk. Back soon. Karen.'

Gone for a walk. They could be anywhere!

She looked at the note again. "Aleisha and I..."

"Aleisha and I?" she said out loud. "Aleisha is with Mom!" A giddy wave of relief swept over her as she realized that Aleisha wasn't in the cave.

"She's safe..."

But if Aleisha was with Karen, who had been calling to Orin in the cave? No, wait, she'd just been imagining that, right?

But Orin was still in the cave. Aleisha was safe; Orin wasn't.

* * *

"She's gone for help," Orin says out loud. "It's okay. She'll be back. Just be calm. Wait..."

He arranges himself in a sitting position against the wall and pulls his knees up under his chin.

The digital display on his watch glows eerily in the inky blackness, and absently he pushes the buttons, flipping through all the functions—time, calendar, stop watch, time in London, New York, Tokyo.

The soft glow, and the fact that everything is working as it should be, gives him some comfort.

But something is moving in the dark.

"Summer?"

Now that he is trying to hear, the darkness is full of sound—his breathing, the thump of his heart, a trickle and plink of water—but not the sound he thought he'd heard, the sound of something moving, grating softly against the rock. There it is again. His heart feels like it has been dipped in ice water.

"Aleisha . . ." His voice catches in his throat.

Nothing . . .

* * *

Summer stumbled against the heavy wooden box that was still sitting in the middle of the workshop floor.

"Aha! That's where it is!" She had been trying to find the flashlight, and now seeing the box she remembered that she had dropped it when she had seen that face at the window. She knelt down and reached under the bench.

"I suppose the batteries are dead," she thought, and they were. "Batteries . . . batteries . . . in the house by the radio . . ."

As she started toward the door, her eye fell on a large coil of plastic rope hanging on a nail. She took it down, slung it awkwardly on one shoulder and headed back toward the house.

She found the new batteries and exchanged them. She dropped the flashlight into her nylon day pack along with the first-aid kit and her Swiss Army knife.

"A note!" she thought. "I should write Mom a note to let her know what's happened."

She sat down at the kitchen table and wrote: "We found a cave by the roots of the fallen tree by the creek. Orin went in, and I am going to find him."

She left the note on the table with a jar of marmalade on one corner to hold it down.

"Where are those two, anyway," she thought. "I'll wait five minutes and then I have got to go. Five minutes ..."

She came back out onto the deck and scanned the meadow and the forest below, willing her mother and her friend to appear. They didn't. She could go on waiting "just five minutes" all afternoon and, as sure as anything, five minutes after she left they'd come back.

She cocked her ear, listening for the sound of approaching feet, for Ralph's bark. She didn't really expect to hear anything ...

*   *   *

The floor of the cave fell away suddenly into a steep chute of rock. She couldn't see Orin, and he wasn't answering her call, but if he'd fallen, he might be unconscious, or (a sharp stab of fear at the thought) he might have wandered further into the cave.

She flipped the coil of rope down into the chute. It slithered down and disappeared from sight. The other end she tied to a root on the fallen tree; Summer jerked the rope as hard as she could and was only slightly reassured when it held; the next time might be the time that the knot slipped or the root broke.

Trying to ignore the possibility, she swung her legs over the edge of the rocks. Sitting there, she realized that she was going to need both hands to hold onto the rope; she wouldn't be able to hold onto the flashlight at the same time. Reluctantly, she switched off the light and pushed it into the pack. She fumbled the pack onto her back, flipped over onto her stomach and started to slide slowly down the slope of rock, paying the rope out a bit at a time. The slope was steep, but not nearly vertical.

"I could climb without the rope if I had to," she thought. "Maybe Orin climbed out, and I missed him somewhere..."

The chute narrowed toward the bottom, and she felt the pack snag against the rock at her back. A story flashed into her mind—a magazine story about a baby who had fallen down a well and had been trapped in the twenty-cm-wide shaft for days and days. She felt a powerful urge to go back, to climb out before it was too late.

Suddenly, she felt her legs slip over an edge and dangle free. She clutched the rope desperately, and tried to picture what was happening. Her upper body was still in the narrow chute, but what was below her? Were her feet hanging a few centimetres above a solid floor, or hanging in the middle of a bottomless abyss?

Could she get back up if she wanted to? She swung her legs, searching for a foothold. Her toes scraped against rock, but there was no crack or ridge to get a hold on. If she was going to get back up, she'd have to use just her arms. She pulled. The thin rope cut into her hands, her knuckles grated against rock, and her body inched upward. Concentrating all her energies, she let go with her right hand, reached up and worked her fingers in under the rope. She took her weight on her right hand and pulled. She didn't move. It was going to be hard to pull her legs up over the edge. She gritted her teeth and pulled again.

All of a sudden, the tension was gone, and she was slipping backwards. She clawed desperately at the rock, but there was no handhold. She was falling.

She didn't fall far, a metre maybe. She landed on her feet first and then sat down hard. After a moment's confusion, she shrugged off the pack and fished out the flashlight. She switched it on.

The light jumped back at her from the rocks pressing close on every side. In two places the darkness swallowed the light—in a black fissure two metres above her head that marked the chute from which she'd fallen, and in a narrow gap to her left.

She played the light over the floor of the cavern, turning slowly as she did so. The immediate area was a scuffed mess, but there were clear footprints in the dust nearby. The zigzag pattern was the kind that would be made by the sole of a running shoe, and...

She knelt down to look more closely, not quite believing her eyes. Beside the running shoe prints were the unmistakeable imprints of bare feet! Her first thought was that Aleisha was in the cave after all, but that didn't make sense.

She moved the beam of the flashlight across the floor of the cavern following the prints in the dust until it shone on—Summer held her breath and stared—a bare foot; two bare feet. Slowly, she moved the light up: two skinny bare legs, a thin body wrapped in a long tunic tied at the waist, thin muscular arms—one held up to shield the eyes from the light—shining white teeth, bared in a grin, and then hair, wild hair, sticking out every which way.

Summer's mind groped for some kind of an utterance, and her mouth opened and closed silently as if she were doing a fish impersonation.

"You're a kid!" Summer croaked. "You're a kid. What are you doing here?"

CHAPTER FOUR . . . in which Nott finally speaks

Summer stood rooted to the spot. The child beckoned to her. Summer shook her head; no, she wasn't going to go with him.

The boy took a step toward her with his hand outstretched. Summer backed away a step and felt the rock behind her.

The child took another step toward her and held up both his hands, palms outward—stop; wait.

He fumbled under his cloak and brought out something which he held out to her. It was Orin's Walkman! The child's other hand moved to his neck. The earphones from the Walkman dangled there. He touched the earphones, then pointed into the dark opening.

"Orin?" said Summer. "You know where Orin is?"

The child bent his knees, and without taking his eyes off Summer's face, put the Walkman down on the dusty floor between them. Then he straightened up and took one step back.

Summer crouched down to pick up the Walkman, watching the child as he had watched her.

"Can you show me where Orin is?" she asked the boy. He stepped into the opening and looked over his shoulder. "Okay," she said. "Let's go."

The boy moved with reassuring certainty through the labyrinth of passageways. After the first two or three turnings, Summer gave up even trying to keep track of where they were going. The air seemed to be getting cooler as they went, but Summer didn't know if that was significant. She pictured herself walking south, further away from the house and the creek, but she knew they could just as easily have been going north or west or around in circles; there was no way of knowing in the darkness.

The boy didn't seem to need the flashlight to find his way, but Summer kept it on, training the beam ahead of her along the floor. A complicated tangle of light and dark pushed ahead of them as the boy's shadow led the way further and further into the cave.

Without warning the boy stopped, and Summer ran into him.

"Oof! Sorry."

The boy turned and pointed to Summer. "What?" asked Summer. "What do you want? What do you mean?" The boy jabbed his finger toward her chest.

"Me..." said Summer. The boy grinned. He pointed toward the ground.

"Me . . . here?" suggested Summer. The boy nodded. He pointed first to himself and then back the way they had just come.

"You go back?" He pointed at her again and again at the ground.

"You're going back; you want me to wait?" The boy nodded emphatically.

"No!" cried Summer. "You can't leave me."

But the boy was gone.

Summer waited for what seemed a long time. "He's coming back," she thought. "He told me to wait . . ."

She switched off the flashlight, thinking to conserve the batteries, but the darkness was too big, too boundless, and she switched it back on again. She felt an almost overwhelming urge to move, to try to find the boy or a way out.

"I'd be lost in a minute," she thought.

Suddenly the ground shook, and she heard or felt a low thump! Her eyes began to sting, and the light from the flashlight seemed to fade. Then she realized that it was dust that was hurting her eyes and killing the light. The tunnel was thick with dust. Before she had time to think about what was happening, the boy materialized out of the swirling gloom. He stepped past her and with a crooked finger, motioned her to follow.

"What happened?" she asked. "Where did you go?"

The boy didn't answer, but she noticed that he was carrying the coil of rope slung across his back. A wave of panic struck her.

"You went back for the rope! Why? What was that noise, and all that dust?"

The boy gave no indication that he even heard her.

"How much farther?" asked Summer.

The boy remained silent.

"How much longer?" she shouted impatiently.

And still the boy walked on in silence.

It occurred to her that she had no sense at all of how long they had already been walking. When she thought about it, it seemed to be a few minutes at most, and then again, hours and hours.

If it had been hours, Karen would have returned home by now, and would have found the note . . .

*   *   *

Karen is on the deck, waving her arms wildly. A Bell Ranger 206B swoops low over the house and drops toward the meadow. ("Orin would be impressed that I remembered the name of the helicopter . . ." The thought intruded for a brief moment and then . . .) Karen runs, slides, lunges down the path toward the meadow. By the time she gets there the three men in orange coveralls have unloaded a small mountain of gear from the storage area behind the passenger compartment. Karen crouches and runs under the spinning rotors to talk with the men. She waves her arms and her mouth moves but no sound can be heard above the noise of the helicopter's motors.

A moment later, the three orange-suited men are jogging along the creek trail toward the fallen tree. They strap crampons on their boots, hook miner's

*lamps on their hats. They rope themselves together
and the first one crawls head first into the cave.*

* * *

The boy stopped again. He put his hand on
Summer's arm and pushed her gently in front of him.
To Summer's surprise, she could see a faint oval of
light ahead. She started toward the light eagerly with
the boy following close behind. A moment later she
stepped out of the cave. She blinked in the bright light
which was pouring from above into a steep walled
canyon. After the darkness and the cool dampness of
the cave, the heat and light beat at her with an
intensity that was almost painful.

On the far side of a small stream a thin wisp of
smoke curled up from a smouldering fire. Someone
was crouched there—very still. The boy strode past
her, waded through the stream and knelt by the fire.
The other person stirred, began to rise. With a start,
Summer realized that it was Orin. He turned to look
at her now, clutching some kind of animal skin
tightly around him, his face smudged with dirt.

"Summer," he said. "What took you so long?"

He was grinning at her.

"Orin, are you okay?" Summer ran to her
friend, splashing through the stream. She threw her
arms around him. When she stepped back, she saw
that, besides the dirt on Orin's face, there was a raw-
looking scrape on one cheek and a large purplish
lump on his forehead. "You're hurt! What happened?"

"Nah, I'm okay," Orin replied. His hand moved
to the lump on his head. "I got a good whack on the

head. I think I might have been out cold for a while. Nott found me in the cave and brought me here."

"Nott?" said Summer. "You mean the boy?"

"I am Nott." The boy spoke for the first time since Summer had seen him.

"So you can talk," said Summer. "I thought maybe..."

"On the far side of the river is the Unknown," continued the boy. "There we cannot speak, and nothing is understood."

"What river?" Summer was becoming more and more confused.

"He means that little stream," whispered Orin.

"The River who brought the Children to the Known," said the boy. "The River who takes our stories. But you will come to know all the stories in time. When you have forgotten, you will begin to know."

"What are you talking about?" asked Summer. She was beginning to feel very uneasy. She had seen people drunk before; she wondered if the boy was on some kind of drug.

But, despite the child's strange way of speaking and his wild appearance, there was a reassuring air of calm authority about him. And despite his size and the smoothness of his face, there was something decidedly un-childlike about him.

"Now I will take you home," said the boy. He gathered up Orin's clothes and handed them to him.

"Your clothes are dry," he said.

At the mention of home, Summer's anxieties evaporated.

"Good," she said. "We should be getting back. Karen will be worried about us. Oh, I didn't tell you—Aleisha *isn't* in the cave. She didn't take your Walkman or the thong."

"I know," said Orin. "He took them." He turned his head toward the boy.

"You?" said Summer. "Why?"

Nott came and crouched by the fire. From inside his cloak he took one end of the thong, the thong that Summer had found hanging on the roots of the fallen tree. As he talked, his fingers caressed the curious objects.

"I crossed the river as I was told. And, as I was told, I walked under the mountain toward where the stories began. I was surprised to find the light—Posil had not spoken of that—but I went toward it. I knew what was there—the Unknown. I was afraid, but my heart beat with excitement, because I knew I was going to see our Mother. I crawled out of the cave, and stood looking about me with wonder. And then..." The boy shuddered at the memory. "...then the beast attacked me. He came from the forest, snarling, and baring his teeth. I fled into the cave, and the beast didn't follow. I was safe, but I had lost the Thread.

"The thread?"

The boy touched the thong.

"It is the Thread, the Thread of our stories, and I am the Keeper of the Thread."

"And I found it," said Summer. "The beast—I bet that was Ralph. I thought he was chasing a squirrel or something."

She remembered the face at the window of the workshop. "And you followed me to get it back, didn't you?"

"I watched you go, and when it was dark, I followed you. I hoped the beast would be asleep . . . "

"That thong, your thread, must be pretty important to you," said Summer. "I mean that must have been pretty scary . . . "

"The Thread binds together the stories of the Children. It binds us to our Mother and to the time before we came here. I was entrusted with its keeping. If I had lost it—" Nott stood up abruptly and walked away from them toward the stream. He knelt there gazing silently into the water.

Summer looked at Orin.

"Weird stuff!" he muttered, shaking his head. "Verrry weird!" Then he shrugged and picked up his clothes. "How about a little privacy," he said to Summer.

She turned around and looked about herself. Steep canyon walls formed a complete circle around them. The stream burbled brightly amongst large rocks and dry, stunted bushes. The boy, Nott, was busy collecting his few utensils into a bundle.

"What happened, Orin?" said Summer, turning her gaze upwards to where the sun was sizzling yellow-white against the pale, hot sky. "I heard you yell, and then I called you. You didn't answer . . . "

"I'm not sure," said Orin. "I guess I banged my head. It was dark. I don't really remember how I got here."

"You said Nott brought you here," said Summer.

"Yeah, he did," said Orin, "I guess. I mean, I don't remember very much. It was really dark. I remember he told me I should take off my wet clothes, because I was shivering, and he made me some kind of tea to drink..."

"You were probably in shock. I think when people are in shock, sometimes they get confused. It looks like you hit your head pretty hard... and you were cold... are you feeling better now?"

"Not too bad," said Orin. "The only thing I need now is music. You can turn around now."

"Oh, I forgot!" said Summer. "Nott gave me this." She handed Orin his Walkman.

"Excellent!" Orin cried.

"We must go now," said Nott. He was speaking to Summer. Orin sat on a rock nearby and fiddled with the tape player.

"Tonight I will pass the Thread to the next Keeper. Are you ready?"

All of a sudden, Orin let out an anguished wail, "Ahhhh!" He snatched the earphones off as if they had burned his ears.

"What's the matter?" cried Summer, taking one step toward him.

"I'll kill her! I'll kill her!" Orin muttered. He tipped his head back and yelled, "Oh, horrid sibling!"

"What? What is it?" asked Summer.

"She switched tapes! I'm lost in the wilderness with a savage gnome and—the loveable monsters of Sesame Street!"

Summer started to laugh. She laughed until the tears ran down her face.

"Hey, it's not funny!"

She laughed so hard she had to sit down. She laughed until her sides ached. Then all at once she stopped laughing. She felt very tired. "I want to go home," she said. "Karen will be wondering where we are."

*   *   *

"Summer! Orin! Are you back yet?" As Karen pushes open the door, Ralph bounds into the room and sideswipes the table. The marmalade jar tips over and rolls across the table. The note lifts in Ralph's wake. It sails gently to the floor and slides under the easy chair in the corner.

Then it is dark, and Karen is running through the bush calling Summer's name. Her clothes are in tatters, her face smeared with dirt. And she is crying.

*   *   *

"Orin, what time is it?" Summer asked. There was a touch of urgency in her voice. "How long have we been gone?"

Orin looked at his watch. "This doesn't make sense!" He squinted up at the sky.

"What?"

"Either I was out cold for nearly twenty-four hours, or my watch has gone berserk." He held out the watch for Summer to see—10:01. "Remember, I looked at it after we fell in the water. It was 10:26."

"I guess it's broken," said Summer.

Orin squinted grimly at the watch and began to

prod at the array of tiny buttons. "Nott," he said, "what time is it?"

The boy hefted his small bundle onto his shoulder. "It is time to go now," said the boy, and as he spoke, strode purposefully toward the wall of the canyon. He stepped around a tall finger of rock and disappeared.

"It seems okay..." muttered Orin, still looking intently at his watch.

Summer pulled him by the arm.

"Come on! He's going!"

Nott led them down through a steep chimney of jumbled stone and out onto a grassy ledge. On one side the ledge fell away into a deep ravine. A steep escarpment rose above and behind them, a soaring wall of red and brown stone. A thin thread of white spun noiselessly from a cleft in the rock and down into the ravine. Summer stood near the edge looking down into the gorge where the ribbon of white spun between tiny boulders.

"Summer, get away from there!" snapped Orin. "You'll fall!"

"It's okay..." said Summer. She liked being up high looking down. A tiny animal—a deer?—was grazing in a small pocket of green at the bottom of the ravine.

"No it's not okay! Get away from the edge!" Orin sounded angry, and Summer realized that he was truly frightened that she might fall.

She stepped away from the edge.

Summer tried to form a picture of where they were in relation to the house, to the creek and the meadow. She couldn't, but somehow, it didn't seem terribly important.

"Come," said Nott. "We will follow the river home."

He led them along the ledge—three tiny black figures moving under the dazzling sun—and down into the forest.

And then it was evening. Their long shadows stalked like giants before them, the whole scene washed a gentle orange by the fading sun.

Summer was tired and hungry. Orin was walking along with his chin on his chest, his eyes half closed, Cookie Monster crooning in both his ears. Nott, though, seemed stronger than ever.

He touched Summer's arm and pointed to several plumes of smoke rising into the sky behind a fringe of trees at the far side of the meadow.

"We are home," he said.

CHAPTER FIVE . . . where they meet the Children of the Known and hear 'The Last Story'

Summer sat on the beaten earth floor. The large, high-ceilinged room was becoming crowded as more and more people, mostly children, came in and took their places, also on the floor. The only light was from torches and candles that were placed near the end of the room at either side of a large flat stone.

"The Keeper of the Thread will sit there," whispered the red-headed boy next to her.

Waiting in the church-like hush of the gloomy hall, Summer tried to think, to make some sense of what was happening to her.

The last few hours—since their arrival in the village—were lost in a blur of strange faces, new smells, and unfamiliar noises.

With some difficulty, Nott had led them through the village, as a crowd—children and a few adults— milled about them crying, "Story! Story!"

Finally, Nott had clambered onto a large boulder and called out, "Please, let us pass. The Children of the Unknown have walked a long way today. You will hear the story. I promise."

At that the crowd had dispersed, and Nott brought them to the door of a large house.

"This is the Keeper's house," he had told them. He ducked past the skin that hung across the entrance. "This is Tagg's house now. I must go soon, but my friend, Tagg, will take care of you."

The boy looked to be about ten years old. He was slightly shorter than Summer. His bright red hair was cropped short and ragged. His face and his arms were covered in freckles. Like Nott, he was dressed in a loose-fitting tunic, tied at the waist, but with what looked like old-fashioned plus-fours underneath. He greeted them with the same confidence and authority that Summer had noticed in Nott.

After a few minutes, Nott bade them farewell, and, with a few whispered words to Tagg, had left the house.

Tagg had arranged for their supper of fish and potatoes and made ready their beds.

"Where did Nott go?" Orin had asked.

"Nott must prepare himself for the Last Story," Tagg replied. "You are puzzled. You don't know about the Last Story, of course. After supper you can come with me to the Rock and see for yourself."

Sitting in the flickering gloom, Summer thought for the twentieth time that afternoon that her mother would be terribly worried. The image of Karen running through the bush came into her mind again and

52

faded instantly. One part of her mind registered surprise that she wasn't more worried about how her mother must be feeling, and then the thought and the image were gone.

"The Keeper is here!" whispered her companion.

Nott was standing there by the rock. The thong was draped across his chest and around his shoulders in much the same fashion as Orin had worn it as a necklace when he had been clowning around earlier in the day.

But Nott wasn't clowning. The silent mood of expectancy in the room told Summer that what she was seeing was very important to Nott and the others.

Nott sat cross-legged on the flat rock, uncoiled the thong from around his neck, and let it fall into his lap. The only sound in the room was the click and skitter of the bones, rocks and other tokens on the thong as they fell against one another.

Then Nott spoke.

"This is the last story that Nott will tell you," he said in a clear commanding voice, "and it is the First Story."

"There was a time, so the First Story tells us, when all children were Children of the Unknown. Those children are remembered now only in the telling of the First Story. Like all Children of the Unknown, they were born tiny and empty of stories. They lived with their mothers who cared for them and watched over them. And like all Children of the Unknown, they grew older and larger

each year until they became mothers themselves. And each year they collected more and more stories. Eventually, they grew too old and their stories grew too many and too heavy to carry. And then they died. That was the way it was, and the way it is, amongst the Unknown."

"He is talking about Orin and me," Summer thought. "We are the Children of the Unknown." She glanced around and saw that all the people in the audience were watching Nott with rapt attention.

"I will tell you now the story of how some of those Children of the Unknown came to the Known and how they forgot.

The summer had been a very hot one. No rain had fallen for many days. The leaves on the trees in the forest and the grasses in the field were brittle and dry. A heavy sleepiness hung on all the land.

One morning, the sun rose, smouldering orange in the sky. The mothers sniffed the air and whispered amongst themselves.

'Fire! Fire! Fire!' The word flickered through the village.

Raven sounded the alarm: 'Fire! Fire! Fire!'

Bear came to warn them that the flames were near.

The air grew hotter and hotter, the sky filled with ash until the sun shimmered ghostly grey. The forest creatures fled in terror.

The mothers gathered the children around them and prepared to leave the village. They ran, but the Fire ran as fast, and faster. At last they came to the River, and stood with their backs to the cool tumbling water as the Fire closed its arms around them.

When the heat was almost too much to bear, one mother, speaking for all the mothers, turned and said to the River: 'Take our children. Care for them and keep them as your own. Better that you should be their mother than they should be devoured by the merciless Fire.'

And so saying, they took the children and hurled them into the water. The River lifted the children up and bore them along past the raging Fire. Angry at having been robbed, the Fire threw tongues of flame across the water and into the forest on the other side. Soon the River was flowing through the very heart of the Fire and its cool waters were starting to hiss and steam.

When it seemed that the children were to be boiled alive, the River reared up and flung itself against the face of a sheer rock wall, splitting it open with a deafening crash. The River flowed into the crack and the children with it. The crack closed behind them, and they were saved.

But, though they had been saved from the tongue and teeth of the Fire, the children were not happy. They wept and keened for the mothers they had left behind in the burning forest.

Seeing how they suffered, the River took pity on them, and calling the children to her, bathed them gently in her waters. The coolness soothed the children and washed away the memories that so tormented them. And in time, they forgot their mothers.

They began to forget, too, the stories that they had brought with them from the Unknown. At last, the new land and the new stories that they told each other there were all that were known to them.

"The Unknown is forgotten and only the Known is known to us."

Nott stood up and slowly started to coil the thong.

"And from that time until this, when a Child of the Known has collected as many stories as he can carry, that Child goes back to the River and bathes again in her waters. Each Child has made the journey many times. And just as the Child of the Unknown is born to the world empty of stories, so when the River has washed him, and he has passed his Forgetting Time, the Child of the Known is empty of stories again. He is born anew."

Nott turned and hung the coiled thong on a peg that projected from the pole behind him. Then he turned again and addressed the waiting group.

"I have made my journey to the River. I will

leave you now to begin my Forgetting Time. When I see you again, Nott will be forgotten except in the stories that you will tell of him. I gave my stories to the River, but three I have kept for you."

He reached inside his tunic and pulled out a thong similar to the one he had just hung up. It was much shorter and only three tokens hung from it. With a small knife he cut the cord that held one of the tokens to the thong.

"This is the story of how Nott dug a hole and water flowed out of it." The token was a small blue stone with a hole drilled through it. He offered it to a boy sitting at the front of the group. "Will you keep this story?"

"I will!" said the boy, taking the token from Nott's hand.

"This . . ." and he removed a second token from the thong. "This is the story of how Nott saved the mother, Bidin, from drowning. Will you keep it, Bidin?" A man with long red hair stood up and picked his way toward the storyteller.

"I will!" he said, as he accepted the token from Nott.

"That is a man, isn't it?" thought Summer. "Why did Nott call him mother?" She turned to whisper the question to Tagg, but the boy was gone.

"And this is the story of how Nott watched in the night and saw the moon being eaten, and how he warned the Children."

The shiny metal disc that Nott removed from his thong was passed to a girl who was sitting on the fringe of the group. With a murmured "I will!" the child accepted the responsibility of preserving the story.

"Now is the time for another to become Keeper of the Thread," said Nott.

Summer was surprised to see Tagg step out of the shadows. The red-headed boy went and stood in front of Nott.

"Remember the stories, Tagg!" said Nott.

"I will!" answered the other.

"Come and ask me my name."

"I will."

"Give me my new name, so that I may become one of the Children of the Known once again."

"I will."

"Then I will go." Nott turned his back and took three deliberate steps away from Tagg. As Nott took the third step, Tagg spoke.

"Nott!" he said. "You leave us with an empty thread and the night is empty. I offer you a story to take with you. Will you choose one?"

Nott turned around.

"I will take a story, and I ask that I might leave another to take its place."

Tagg stepped to the peg, uncoiled the thong and held it out to Nott. "Choose."

Nott fingered the talismans that dangled from the thong. Finally, his fingers closed around one of them, and with his knife he cut the cord that held the token to the thong. He slipped the token into his tunic.

"Thank you," he said.

"You have taken a story for yourself," said Tagg.

"Tell us the story that you would have us keep in its place." Still holding the thong, he stepped into the shadows as Nott climbed onto the flat rock and sat cross-legged, looking out at the faces of his friends and inward at the pictures that he was about to describe to them.

"This is my story of how the Keeper of the Thread brought the two children, Summer and Orin, through the mountain from the Unknown."

CHAPTER SIX...in which Summer discovers that the story is true, and she makes a plan

Orin was sitting in front of a teepee surrounded by half a dozen children. One of the children was wearing Orin's earphones and was laughing nervously. The others were watching with a mixture of amusement and apprehension.

"They've never heard anything like this!" called Orin. "Can you imagine if it was 'The Allergic Reactions'? It would blow them away!"

"Tagg is showing me around the village," Summer called back. "Do you want to come?"

"Later! We're having a good time here!"

"How's your head?" Tagg asked.

"Fine!" said Orin. The swelling was gone. Only a slight yellowy splotch showed where he'd bumped himself.

"See you in a while!" Summer called.

They left Orin and his group of new friends and walked through the village toward the river.

"Over there is where we store the roots and berries that we collect and the vegetables we grow. And those huts are the smoke houses. The River gives us fish in abundance. We dry some and smoke some, for those times—like the Forgetting Times—when we have to be away from the River. It tastes good, too, the smoked fish."

A flock of geese honked and flapped across their path, driven by two children carrying long willow whips that they used to tickle the animals along when they strayed or dawdled.

They passed a hut where a child and an adult were sitting on the ground, working intently.

"Erl and the mother, Sind, are repairing clothes there. Erl is very clever with a needle. He will teach Sind." Tagg turned away from the river path and led Summer through a patch of low bushes toward a bare knob of rock a short distance away.

"I will show you now where the tools are kept," said the boy.

"Why do you keep them so far from the village?" asked Summer. "Wouldn't it be handier to have them close to where you are working?"

"I will show you," the boy answered, smiling broadly. He was enjoying showing off the treasures of the village to the newcomer.

They climbed up the moss-covered slope of exposed stone, stepped from rock to rock down the far side and into a deep hollow. There a young girl sat on a stool, apparently guarding a heavy wooden door set into the rock.

"I have not come to borrow a tool, Hana," said Tagg. "I would simply like to show Summer where we keep them. Summer, this is Hana. She is one of the Children whose job it is to care for the tools."

"Hello, Hana," said Summer.

Hana smiled, and turned to open the door.

"See," said Tagg. "It is dry and cool, and safe. A perfect place to store the tools!"

In the light that spilled through the open door, Summer could see that the tool storage was, in fact, a natural cave in the rock. Along each wall for several metres, back to where the fissure dwindled to a point, an odd assortment of tools was arranged on rough shelves. Summer could see axes, hatchets, two bucksaws, a plane, and screwdrivers.

A coil of yellow polypropylene rope lay on one of the shelves. Summer, assuming it was hers, started to ask how it had come to be there. She realized before she spoke, though, that the question might sound like an accusation, so she left it unsaid.

"It's probably not mine anyway," she thought as she turned her attention to the other items on the shelf.

There were knives, whetstones, wrenches, a carpenter's level, several rifles, and many things whose function Summer could not even begin to guess at.

"They are curious things, are they not?" said Tagg. "The knives we know how to use. And the fishing tools..."

He showed her a collection of fish hooks and lures arranged on a pelt on one of the shelves.

"We have used pieces of the old tools to make new fishing tools. See?" He showed her a fish hook that had been fashioned from an old spring.

A half a dozen hatchets and axes were laid out neatly on a shelf. They, at least, seemed well used and cared for.

"These are axes," Tagg said. "They are used for chopping wood. You can cut down a tree even."

"I know," said Summer. She noticed, toward the back of the shelf, an axe that had been left to rust. It had a large head, flat on one side and bevelled on the other. Larry had had one like it in his workroom.

"You don't use this one?" she said.

"It looks like an axe of some kind, but it chops poorly. See it is flat on one side . . ."

"It's called a broad-axe," she said. "It's used for flattening off the side of logs, so they fit together better."

Tagg frowned.

"My dad had one like that." She remembered how Larry had been determined to build their house just as the pioneers had built theirs—every timber hand-hewn, wooden pegs instead of nails. He had hunted for weeks to find a broad-axe, but after hacking away all day to flatten off just one big log, he had gone back to using the chainsaw.

"I could show you how it works . . ."

Tagg frowned again, and shook his head.

"Really. I don't think it's too hard . . ."

At that moment Hana stepped into the tool room.

"Tagg," she said. "Can you come?" Her voice carried a note of urgency.

Summer reached out with both hands and picked up the broad-axe. She could picture in her mind exactly where Larry's had hung on the workroom wall. She could smell the oil and dust of the workroom. She could see Larry there, bent over his chainsaw, sliding the file carefully over each tooth...

* * *

Summer is sitting propped against a fence post at the side of the road. Her arm is in a sling and a grey wool blanket is tucked around her.

The Huey thuds close overhead, the wind from the rotors swirling the dust into her eyes. The truck driver is running toward the machine as it lowers itself into the field above the road. Now two men have jumped to the ground from the big door in the side of the helicopter. Summer can see them waving their arms and moving their lips, but all sound is swallowed in the wash of noise from the powerful engines.

Now the pilot is out of the machine and talking with the others. One of the first two men goes back to the machine, and the pilot heads towards her.

Strangely, it isn't relief, but alarm, that she feels when she recognizes the pilot.

"It's Orin's dad!" she thinks. "He'll tell Karen. She'll be really upset."

But he's here now and he's talking to her.

"I'm going to take you over to the chopper now, Summer," he says kindly. "We're going to fly you and Larry down to Smithers to the hospital."

"Is he going to be okay?" asks Summer.

"That'll be for the doctor to say," he tells her. "Okay, hold your arm as still as you can while I lift you up."

"I'm really sorry!" she says, as he carries her toward the helicopter.

"Hey, it's not your fault," he says.

"Yes, it is!" cries Summer. "If I hadn't made him take me to the horse show, it wouldn't have happened!"

"It just happened," says Orin's dad soothingly.

Summer doesn't say anything, but over and over in her mind she repeats it: "I'm sorry! I'm sorry! I'm sorry..."

"Do you feel strong enough to sit up?" Orin's dad asks her. And when she nods, "Why don't you sit up front with me."

He leaves her sitting in the cockpit of the helicopter and disappears. Then, through the side window she can see the four men running toward her each carrying one corner of the stretcher. The person on the stretcher is covered with a grey blanket, even his face.

* * *

"I have to go," said Tagg. "Hana will show you the tools."

He picked up the coil of rope.

66

"The rope that you brought us," he said, "it might be useful. I will take it..."

Although she had not intended the rope to be a gift, it pleased Summer to think that her "gift" was appreciated.

"They can keep it," she thought

"Where are you..." she started to ask, but Tagg was gone.

"Where is he going?" Summer asked Hana.

"You are crying," said Hana, either not hearing, or choosing to ignore the question. "Are you alright?"

Summer hadn't been aware of the tears on her face. She wiped them away on the sleeve of her shirt.

"I was just remembering something," she said.

"Ah... soon you will forget." The girl's voice was soothing. "Soon you will not cry."

"I'm not crying now," said Summer, putting the axe back on the shelf. "Tell me where you got all these things. Where did this come from?"

She picked up a small leather box inside of which was nestled an ornate brass compass.

"I do not know," said Hana. "All the tools were brought here by children and mothers who came from the Unknown, but I do not know their stories. Perhaps the Keeper of the Thread knows, but I think that even he has forgotten."

"This is a really neat old thing," said Summer. "Couldn't we ask the person who brought it?"

"The mother who brought that, or the child—he does not know. The River took his stories. He now has only the stories that he has learned here. His old name and his old stories are gone now." Summer remembered the stories that she had heard the night before.

"You mean that that business about the river washing away memories—that really happens?"

"Of course," said Hana.

"It's not just a story?"

"It is a story, yes. But it really happens."

"But why don't you just stay away from the river?" asked Summer. "I mean if it makes you forget, why don't you . . . "

"You will understand when you have been among us long enough, Summer," said Hana. "There will come a time when the burden of the stories will become heavy to you as well, and you will be happy to give them to the River."

"I don't believe that!" said Summer. "Nobody wants to forget. I know what happens to old people, they start to forget things . . . "

"And then they die . . . " said Hana. "That is what the first story says

. . . and each year they collected more and more stories. Eventually, they grew too old and their stories grew too many and too heavy to carry. And then they died.
But here, no one grows old. The River takes away the stories, so that they never become a burden."

"No one grows old? That's crazy! Everybody grows old. What about Bidin and Sind and the other mothers? They're older than you."

"Bidin and the others are the same now as they

68

were when they came to the Known. You, too, will stay the same as you are now."

"What about babies? Do your babies stay babies all their lives?"

"...When I was a Child of the Unknown, I was born to the world a shrunken, stupid thing, unable to walk, to speak or to feed myself. Wolves of the forest stalked my bed and I could not run. I screamed for my Mother, and if she did not come, I died helpless, helpless..."

Summer realized that the girl was quoting from one of the stories.

"But babies grow up," she protested. "They're not always helpless..."

"When a Child of the Known is born, he is born whole. If the Wolf stalks his bed, he can run, or he can kill the Wolf. Thanks to the River, and her kindness, no Child need ever cry for his Mother again."

"Are you saying that there are no babies here?" Now that she thought of it, Summer couldn't remember seeing either babies or old people in the village.

"No, there are no babies," said Hana.

"Are you seriously saying that you always stay the same? You never change?"

"The stories change. There are new stories all the time. We collect our stories, and we give them back, and we collect them again. And so it goes forever."

"But if you never change, that means that you never die!" said Summer.

"Of course..."

"Nobody dies?"

"Nobody grows old, and nobody dies," said Hana.

Summer left the cool shadows of the cave and climbed up over the knob of rock again. The sun, halfway up the sky, seemed to hiss and sizzle against the faded blue. The heat pressed against Summer's skin like a feverish hand. Below her the forest and the village, the river and the hills, wavered as if seen through water or imperfect glass.

Thoughts boiled in her brain as if her head was a kettle and the sun the fire.

"Nobody dies..."

Summer sat on a rock. People moved in the village below her; the green panorama of forest stretched to the vaguely shimmering hills and mountains. But what Summer was watching was the tumbling confusion of images in her mind. She watched and didn't even try to make sense of it. And eventually, the tumbling slowed and patterns emerged. One picture flowed into another. It seemed cooler now. Then one picture... light playing softly through a tangle of greenery on a window sill... there were voices...

*   *   *

Karen watches with satisfaction as Hana's fingers twirl the wool skilfully into a thin strand.

Karen looks over at Summer and smiles.

"She learns fast. Soon we will be ready to begin weaving the cloth."

Hana smiles too. "I am glad you came here, Karen, to show us how to spin and weave."

"I have to go and help Tagg repair that harness," says Summer. "We want to skid some more logs in to start work on Nott's new house."

As she goes out the door, Sind comes hurrying up to her. "Summer!" he calls. "One of the cows seems to be unwell. Can you come and look at her?"

As she hurries off toward the pasture, she sees Aleisha playing with two of her friends near the well. Orin is nearby showing one of the children how to work a mill that he has built to grind corn into flour.

It is evening now. Summer sits with Karen on the pounded dirt in front of the stone, where the Keeper of the Thread is gently touching the stories hung from the thong. He selects one and begins to speak.

"I am going to tell you the story of Summer, who came to the Known and taught us how to use the tools..."

Karen takes one of Summer's hands in hers, and gives it a gentle squeeze. Summer looks down and thinks that her mother's hands have always been the same—small with stubby fingers, rough and work-worn, but gentle and skilful and strong.

"They have always been like that," she thinks,

"and they will be that way always, because here in the Known all things stay the same... and nobody dies."

CHAPTER SEVEN...in which Nott is broken and the children hide from THE BOATMAN

"You're going to burn your skin, sitting like this in the sun."

Summer turned quickly to see Hana climbing up behind her. The girl stood shading her eyes against the strong sun, looking intently away along the river.

"Who's the leader here, Hana?"

Hana gave her a puzzled look.

"If I was wanting to talk to someone about something important, who would be the best person?"

"The Keeper of the Thread knows more stories than any of the other Children..." said Hana. She answered hesitantly, and it seemed to Summer she didn't quite understand the question.

"I'll tell you what I've been thinking..." said Summer. "I've been thinking that it might be a good idea if we stayed here, Orin and me. I'd get my mom to come too, and we could live here with you guys. We could be a big help. We could show you how to use the tools in there, and when Karen comes she could bring a lot of the stuff from our house..."

"No!" said Hana. "It cannot be. You will forget all that. The tools, your mother—they are of the Unknown..."

"But you can do a lot of things with the tools that you can't do with your hands. I could show you."

"No! You cannot."

"But why?"

"The tools are of the Unknown..."

"Why bother keeping them, if you're not going to try to learn how to use them?"

"The tools are powerful. Those that are known to us we may use, but those that are unknown must stay here, so that they will remain unknown. It is my job to see that only those that are known are used by the Children."

"I don't understand why you guys worry so much about the Unknown. It's not horrible there."

"The Children of the Unknown grow old. They suffer and die."

"Why did Nott bring us here?" Summer's voice betrayed the exasperation she was feeling. "If everything about the Unknown is so scary..."

Hana frowned and fidgeted uncomfortably. "He should not have brought you here!" she said. "He should not have taken your friend's music tool. He was very foolish. He should not have told the story."

Summer turned and walked away from Hana.

The girl didn't want them there. Did they all feel that way? No, Tagg had seemed friendly enough. Could it be that they really didn't want to learn how to use the tools? Didn't they realize how much easier life would be if they did learn?

Summer thought of how she had seen herself as the hero of the story—"Summer, who came to the Known and taught us how to use tools..." —and she felt foolish, then angry. "To heck with them!" she muttered under her breath. But if what she said was true about nobody dying... and maybe Hana was wrong about the tools...

"Hana," she said, turning, "I didn't mean to upset you about the tools. When I get home, I want to talk to Karen—that's my mom—and if she would like to come here and live..."

"This *is your home*, Summer. Soon you will forget the place that was your home."

So it was okay—they were welcome after all!

"Thank you," said Summer. "I think I would like this to be my home. I won't forget my old home, of course..."

"Oh, but you will. You must. Even now you are beginning to forget. You will go for your Forgetting Time, and when you return you will have a new name. You will be one of the Children of the Known."

"I won't forget everything. I won't forget Aleisha and Lynn!"

"You will collect new stories..."

"But I don't want to forget—not everything!"

"You have given your stories to the River. As

75

soon as you crossed the river, the Forgetting began..."

"We have to go back then! Nott has to take us
back!"

"Nott has gone away, Summer, to his Forgetting
Time. When he comes back to the village, he will
come with a new name, and he will have forgotten all
that he knew as Nott."

"No, we have to go back... back to the Unknown!"

Hana wasn't listening. She was looking down
toward the village, shielding her eyes from the sun
with one hand.

"Danny is coming. He is running."

Summer could see the small figure hurrying
toward them.

"He has news."

"What news?" asked Summer.

But the girl was gone, running down the path
toward the boy. They met and talked together, the
boy waving his arms and pointing back toward the
village. Then, without even a glance in Summer's
direction, they sprinted away along the path.

Pushing away a suffocating feeling of loneliness,
Summer started slowly down the hill, but not toward
the village—whatever was going on there had nothing to do with her.

Summer walked toward the river and along the
river bank. Two children were fishing from the bank
with long poles. Two others were working swiftly
and deftly, gutting and filleting the fish that had been
caught. They seemed unaware of the thick clouds of

flies that buzzed around their heads and crawled on their hands. They seemed unaware, too, of the large grey and white birds that hovered, screeching, above them, waiting to swoop down to snatch a meal from the glistening pile of discarded heads and guts and bones. The smell was horrible.

"That's not a job for kids," she thought. And then she realized that they weren't kids; they looked like kids, but if what Hana said was true, they were actually old... how old?

She watched their hands moving—a quick slit along the belly, a smooth scooping motion to remove the guts, a slit along the backbone and then the knife sliding down, peeling the meat away from the ribs— skilled hands, old hands.

* * *

The girl's hands work swiftly, cutting, scooping, peeling. Beside her a blond boy is working with quick, sure movements.

The boy turns to the girl, and speaks.

"Nearly done, Sami," he says. "We have done well today."

"I am finished, Newt," she says. She stands and goes to wash her hands in the river. The face that looks back at her from the rippled surface of the water is Summer's face.

* * *

"We have to go home!" She didn't know how, but she knew certainly, without question, that was what they had to do. She had to find Orin. And together, they had to find Nott.

She found Orin easily enough. He was sitting

alone in front of Tagg's house, cross-legged on the grass, his earphones on.

"Orin!"

"You don't have to shout," he said, taking the earphones off.

"Orin, we have to talk. We have to make plans."

"The batteries are dead! I don't suppose there's a corner store around here somewhere."

"It doesn't matter about the music," she said. "We have to go, Orin. We have to go back home before we forget."

Suddenly, a short child with a round face and a round little body came bustling up to them. He was carrying a rough basket full of food—vegetables, dried fish, a pouch of dried berries.

"You better collect yourself some food," he panted. "And some firewood. You won't want to be going hungry when the Boatman comes."

"What are you talking about?" asked Summer.

"The Boatman is coming," said the boy. "Nott got broken. Three days we won't be able to go out. You better get some food."

"Nott? What happened to Nott?" asked Summer. She felt cold in the pit of her stomach. She remembered the boy who had come to fetch Hana. "Is he hurt?"

"He's broken!" said the child as he bustled away.

Summer hadn't noticed as she came through the village: something was happening. There was a sense of urgency about the way people were moving. Others, besides the fat boy, were carrying baskets of

food. In front of a nearby house, one of the mothers sitting on the ground was crying. A child stroked his hair and tried to comfort him.

"Will the Boatman take me away?" whimpered the mother. "I'm scared!"

"It's okay," the child soothed. "You'll be all right. As long as we stay in the house you'll be safe."

The mother rocked back and forth and groaned softly.

"Orin," said Summer. "What's going on?"

"I don't know. I only know that if I don't get some new batteries, I'm sunk."

Summer spotted Hana hurrying by with a basket of food. She caught up with her and grabbed her arm.

"Hana!"

The girl stopped and turned.

"Hana," said Summer. "What is happening? Everybody is rushing around collecting food. And a boy told me Nott was broken. Did he break a leg or what? What did he mean?"

"He was on his way to the Forgetting Place," said Hana, "and he fell. He broke on the rocks."

"What did he break?" asked Summer. "Is he badly hurt?"

"He broke..." She stopped and seemed to be searching for an answer to the question. "He broke himself. Nott is broken. He cannot be fixed."

"You mean he's..." Summer didn't want to ask the question, because she was afraid that she already knew the answer. "Is he dead?"

"He is not dead!" snapped Hana. Her eyes snapped, too. "He is broken. The Children of the Known cannot die."

"But you said . . . "

"The mountains cannot die, but even they can be broken. Only the Water cannot be broken."

"He's dead," whispered Summer.

"He is broken!" declared Hana, turning and walking swiftly away.

But Nott *was* dead. His body lay on the same flat stone where he had sat the previous evening. Again, the only light in the rough hall was provided by torches and candles on either side of the rock. The waiting crowd was eerily silent.

Tagg stepped out of the shadows behind the rock and stood solemnly surveying the faces in the crowd.

"Nott has been broken," he said.

A soft murmur ran through the crowd.

"He has been broken and cannot be mended. I will tell you a story.

"I have told and you have told and we have all heard how the River brought the children to the Known place, and how we keened for memory of the mother that we left behind. You have told and I have told and we have all heard how the River pitied the children and called them to her. She took their stories away so that they would forget their mothers and would not suffer.

The River called the Children to her.

Two children, though, did not heed the call. They left the others to search for a way back. They searched to east and west. They walked to the south and again to the north. On all sides they found their way blocked, here by a wall of sheer rock, there by dense forest, on one hand by an impassable swamp and on the other by high crags amongst which the River boiled and hissed as if filled with fire.

They searched for many days.

They told each other the old familiar stories, but as each day passed and obstacle after obstacle reared up in their paths, the stories became more and more tinged with pain and longing.

One day, they came to a place where high walls blocked their way once more.

'I can hear her calling to us,' said the younger child. 'Can you hear her calling?'

'I can hear the wind,' said the other.

'No, it is our mother,' said the first. 'She is waiting at the top. If we can only climb...'

The child began to climb. Slowly, she inched her way up the stone face, fingers and toes finding a purchase where the eye denied that any was.

And then she fell. She fell amongst the rocks, and was broken.

The older child picked her up and carried her to the River. He told the River how the child had searched for a way to return to her mother, and how she had been broken in the search.

He pleaded with the River to take the child back. 'She cannot suffer more, be she here or there,' replied the River. 'I will take her back. But all her stories must go with her. Is it agreed? Then build a boat to carry her, and when it is ready, place her in it.'

In three days, the child built a boat. He laid the broken child in it. The River lifted up the boat and carried all away—the boat, the child and her stories.

The boatman did not return to the company of the other children. He lived at the edge of the Known, in the shadow of the rocks.

He lives there still. He practices his craft along the river, waiting for a passenger to ride the boats he builds. He haunts the forest paths waiting for another to whom he can teach his art, for then, and only then, will he be able to go to the River and give her his stories.

"He will come now to take another broken child. He will build a boat and place in it the child we called Nott, Nott and all his stories."

Three figures approached the rock—the mother, Bidin, and the two children to whom Nott had entrusted his stories the evening before. Each, in turn, placed a token in the Keeper's hand and returned to the group.

"Within the next three days, the Boatman will come. For three days, you must hide yourselves, lest the Boatman take you for his apprentice. Go to your houses. The Boatman is coming."

CHAPTER EIGHT...where Summer and Orin run
away to build a raft

"We need to talk to Tagg," said Summer. "We
need to know if those things Hana told me are true."

Following Tagg's warning about the Boatman,
the Children had gone quietly through the gathering
twilight to their houses and tents. Now, lying on their
sleeping mats in the shadows of the Keeper's house,
Summer and Orin were alone for the first time since
Summer had found out about Nott's accident.

"Hana said there's no way to go home," said
Summer softly, speaking as much to herself as to
Orin. "She said that we are already starting to forget.
If she was right..."

"I never forget a thing!" declared Orin. "I've got
a mind like a steel trap."

"Let's do a test," said Summer, sitting up and addressing the dark lump against the wall. "What's your name—your whole name?"

"This is silly," protested Orin. "That's all just stories, about forgetting things."

"Maybe," said Summer. "But answer the questions. What's your whole name."

"Orin Baxter Webb."

"Where do you live?"

"In Vancouver, and in the summer..."

"Alright, let me ask you something hard," interrupted Summer.

"Who is the drummer for 'The Basket Cases'?"

That was one of Orin's favourite bands; Summer had never actually listened to them.

"That's easy," said Orin. "His name is... I mean her name..."

"Wait, that's too hard," said Summer. "I don't know why I asked you that—I don't even know the answer myself. Here's another one."

"Ask me another music question."

"Okay. What was the last concert you saw in Vancouver?"

"I think it was 'Toad and the Holes'... no that was way before my birthday. It was... I forget, Summer. I forget!"

"You're probably just tired."

"It's not like me to forget something like that," said Orin.

"No it's not like you," said Summer. "And that's the thing, Orin—if Hana was right and you do forget

86

what you know, you're not you anymore. I wonder how much I'm forgetting..."

"I can't remember the identification numbers on Dad's machine. I know that number. I know I know it..."

"What if we are forgetting? We just can't let it happen. What are we going to do?"

"If Hana was telling the truth, there's nothing we can do, is there? She said there's no way to go home."

"There has to be a way," said Summer. "There has to be."

Night sounds of frogs and running water seeped into the house to fill the silent spaces around them, as the two children sat listening to their own thoughts.

"There are some things I wouldn't mind forgetting," said Orin. "Before Mom took us to Vancouver, she and Dad fought a lot. Mom didn't like living out in the bush, but Dad couldn't understand that. He was always busy building or getting in the winter wood supply, or sharpening his saw. That's what made him happy. But Mom said he liked his bloody chainsaw better than he liked her. One day Mom got so mad, she threw the chainsaw down the outhouse hole. We thought Dad was going to slug her! Aleisha was screaming, and everything..."

Summer was quiet for a long time.

"I thought about that, too," she said at last. "About how it would be good to forget some things. It was my fault, you know... the accident. If I hadn't been bugging Larry to get to that stupid horse show on time..."

"That's crazy," said Orin. "It was just an accident! Accidents happen!"

"No! It wasn't just an accident! It was my fault. And I can never forget that..."

"You could—you would—if you stayed here," said Orin. "I'm not saying you should..."

"It would be nice, not to have to think about it ever, ever again. I hate it when someone mentions Larry, and those pictures start in my head. I keep seeing the accident over and over again," said Summer. "But what about all the other people we love? Staying here and forgetting about them—that would be almost the same as if they died, too."

"Not really..."

"We can't do it. We can't just let our family and our friends fade away."

"But if we have no choice, why fight it?" said Orin.

"We have to try," insisted Summer. "We don't know if Hana was telling us the truth. We just don't know! Maybe if we could talk to Tagg..."

"He didn't come back with us after the story. And we need to stay inside for three days."

"We can't wait that long! We have to find a way home."

"Okay," said Orin, "let's. What are we going to do?"

"I don't know, for sure, but something tells me the river is our best bet. I know we couldn't find our way back through the caves, and the river has to go somewhere."

"We're going to swim?"

"We're going to build a raft. I have my Swiss Army knife, and we have the rope... or do we? I wonder if Tagg put it back?"

Summer got up and began feeling her way about in the dark.

"Where's the other stuff I brought?"

"I don't know," said Orin.

"The tool place," said Summer. "Someone must have taken it to put in the tool place. Come on! We have to get them back. We can't build a raft with our bare hands." She grasped Orin's wrist and pulled him toward the doorway.

"We're not going to go now, are we?" he protested. "What about the Boatman. What if the Boatman sees us?"

"Don't think about it," said Summer. She pushed Orin out past the hide that covered the door.

As she had hoped, Hana, too, had gone to her tent to await the coming of the Boatman. Her little stool was tipped against the door—a sort of token barricade.

Summer opened the door. Inside was total darkness. She groped about trying to visualize where things were. Screw-drivers... yes. The saw was on the shelf just below that...

"How did you know this was here?" asked Orin.

"Tagg showed me this place earlier today," said Summer. "They keep all their tools here. It's kind of like a communal tool kit." Her hand scraped against something sharp. "Ow! I found the saw... Here! Can you hold it?" She held the saw out toward the black lump behind her. Orin put out his hand, and after a bit of waving about, managed to connect with the saw.

"Hey! Look what I found!"

"What?" asked Orin.

"If it works..." muttered Summer. Orin clamped his eyes shut against the sudden glare of the flashlight.

With the help of the flashlight, they were soon able to find Summer's pack with the first-aid kit and the Swiss Army knife still inside.

"Thank goodness, he brought the rope back! We'll take the saw," said Summer, "and this axe. And we might as well take this."

"What is it?"

"A compass."

"Is this stealing?" said Orin.

"If it gets us home, I don't care," said Summer. "And if it doesn't, I guess we're part of the group, and we are allowed to use the tools if we want. Too bad there are no nails... we'll have to make do with just the rope."

"Where to now?" asked Orin.

"We need to get some food," said Summer. "I know where the root cellar is."

"You sure get around, don't you!" said Orin.

They started out following the river bank but were soon forced by thick bushes growing right down to the water's edge to circle away from the river and into the confusing tangle of moon-laced trees.

Pushing through the underbrush was hard work. Even with the flashlight to show the way, they were constantly tripping on exposed roots, snagging their clothes and being slapped in the face with branches. Eventually, they stumbled onto a well-worn path.

"Great!" said Orin breathlessly. "No more hacking our way through the bush."

"I don't know if it's a good idea to stay on the path," said Summer. "We don't even know where it leads. And someone might come along."

"Everyone is in their tents for three days."

"Alright," said Summer. "Let's follow the path for a while. It seems to go along beside the river..."

They walked on.

"How far are we going?" said Orin. "I thought we were going to build a raft and float home, not walk the whole way."

"We should get away from the village," Summer replied, "... just in case."

"Just in case what?" said Orin. "Come on! What's wrong with this place?"

"The bank is too steep here," said Summer. "We need a flat place, so we can lay the logs down."

"The first flat place we come to, I'm stopping!" said Orin, plodding on ahead.

Summer trudged after him feeling very weary.

* * *

The Boatman is sitting on a fresh stump watching her with his small black eyes. He is twining the end of his long white beard in his fingers and grinning.

"You're doing good," he says. "A few thousand more trees and we'll have enough wood to build a proper ship. Get at it."

Summer picks up her axe. It's so heavy and her arms are so tired that the axe seems to be stuck to the ground like a giant magnet stuck on a ball of iron. But she lifts it.

All around her are the trunks of the hundreds of trees that she has had to cut down, and ahead of her the forest stretches on and on to the mountain wall. She knows that the Boatman expects her to cut them all.

"I'm tired," she says. "And my hands are all blistered."

"No complaining now!" says the Boatman. "You signed on of your own accord. No one said the work would be easy."

"I didn't!" said Summer. "I didn't sign on for anything!"

"They told you to stay inside. You didn't stay inside."

* * *

"A flat place!" said Orin. "I'm stopping!"

He sat down on a fallen tree and started to open the bundle of food that they had found in the supply cache.

"Yeah," said Summer, "this is a good place." A wide gravel bank separated them from the river. "Let's have some food and then we can get started."

She sat down beside Orin on the log. But then even sitting seemed too much effort. She slithered down to the ground and leaned back against the log with her eyes shut.

CHAPTER NINE...in which Orin doesn't hear Summer call, "Timber!"

"Duncan. Bloomfield. Hidber."

"Which Hidber? Young or old? Carl or John?"

"John. Next is Takito's. Then Hoff's. Then Carl Hidber. Flint. Tyler down Bruce Road. Then us and then you. How did I do?"

"You missed the Johnson family," said Summer. "But they moved in last winter when you were away, so that doesn't really count."

Orin was naming all the families along the road that ran from the highway up to Summer's place. Summer had a theory that if they kept reviewing everything they knew about themselves they wouldn't forget.

"Ask me something," she said.

The first tree they tackled was about thirty centimetres across. Orin started the first cut on the side of the tree closest to the river.

"Might as well fell it as close as we can," he reasoned.

"I think you should stop and start a new cut now," Summer said when he was part way through the trunk. "We should cut out a kind of wedge."

"I know that," said Orin. "I've cut down trees before. Just a little deeper."

The tree uttered a tiny high squeal and settled over ever so slightly, clamping the saw blade tight. Orin muttered something under his breath and tugged angrily at the saw. But it wouldn't come loose.

He cursed and kicked at the trunk, and finally sat down on the ground, scowling at his running shoes.

"We'll have to use the axe," said Summer. "We can cut from the other side, and then, when the tree falls, we'll be able to get the saw out. It's no big deal."

She picked up the axe and started to work.

"Let me," said Orin.

"I can do it," said Summer. She knelt down on the ground, wiped her hand on her jeans and took a fresh grip on the axe handle. "I just have to widen out the cut."

Orin shrugged his shoulders. "Well, call me if you need some help," he said.

By the time she had carved a ten centimetre deep notch into the tree, Summer's fingers were beginning to feel sore and her legs were uncomfortably cramped. She stood up and stretched. She looked around for Orin, but couldn't see him. With a sigh, she settled back to the task.

Twice, she decided that the cut was deep enough, that all that was needed was for her to give the tree a good push. Both times, the tree rocked hardly at all despite her straining and grunting. And each time, when she went back to chopping, the axe seemed heavier and the wood tougher.

"Okay, tree, down you go!" she said at last, standing and wiping the sweat out of her eyes. She leaned against the trunk and pushed. It started to move, and Summer stepped back, knowing that the butt could kick back and hit her if she wasn't careful. And just then, she caught a glimpse of Orin's bright shirt. He was walking right under the tree.

"Look out!" she yelled. "Timber!"

The tree tilted over slowly, slowly and then faster, faster—twisting as it fell. Summer saw a blur through the underbrush and heard a metallic twang as the saw blade twisted and then sprang into the air in a crazy little cartwheel. There was a gnashing of broken limbs and torn branches, a heavy thump and then quiet.

"Orin!" Summer called. She started to run toward the spot where she had seen his shirt, and almost tripped over Orin sitting on the ground nursing a scraped arm. "Are you alright?" she asked.

"Aren't you supposed to yell 'timber' or something?" he replied testily.

"I did," cried Summer.

"Yeah. After the tree was three quarters of the way to the ground!"

"I'm sorry. Are you hurt? I didn't see you. Really."

"Yeah, I'm okay," said Orin. "I suppose I was being a bit careless, too. Oh, no!"

"What?" asked Summer.

"Look!" Orin held out his arm. His fancy wrist-watch was smashed, the glass crumbled. "How are we going to know the time in Tokyo?"

"We don't need to know the time in Tokyo," said Summer. "The important thing is that you're . . ."

Orin jumped up suddenly and yelled, "I need to know the time in Tokyo! I need to know! It's important to *me*!" He fumbled the watch off his wrist and threw it as far as he could into the bush. He stomped off toward the river.

Summer watched him go. She considered going after him, but thought better of the idea and walked back to where she'd dropped the axe. Grim-faced, she began stripping the branches off the tree.

A while later, Orin came back and picked up the saw.

"How big are we making this raft?" he said.

Summer stopped chopping and turned to look at him. "I'm sorry about your watch," she said. "I know it was important to you."

"Let's build the boat," said Orin. "The sooner we get back the better. Two metres? Three?"

"Two, I guess," said Summer. "Two should be long enough."

They worked in silence for a while, Summer hacking the branches off the tree, Orin beginning to cut the first length of trunk.

"It's not just the watch," said Orin. "That was an expensive watch, but it was . . . more than that. It's like now, with the watch gone maybe I will forget that Tokyo even existed, and London and . . ."

"And home?"

By early the next afternoon, a dozen poles, each about two metres long, were floating in a backwater formed by a gravel bar that swept in a wide arc out into the river. Summer and Orin were working thigh-deep in the water lashing the poles together.

"Tell me all the birthdays of all the people in your family including all cousins, aunts, and grand-parents," said Orin.

"I couldn't remember birthdays before we came here!" said Summer. "Ask me something else."

"We're not going to have enough rope," said Orin.

"How many logs do you think it is going to take?" asked Summer.

"I don't know," said Orin. "They're pretty skinny..."

"I know," said Summer. She waded ashore and got the knife out of her pack. She waded back and took the rope out of Orin's hands. She cut the end and started to untwist the three strands that made up the thicker strand. "Now we have three times as much."

"Will it be strong enough?" asked Orin.

"Sure. Hey, I was thinking, instead of just tying the logs together side by side, we should cut a cross piece for each end and tie the logs onto that."

"Good idea!" said Orin wading ashore. "How long for the cross piece? How about a metre? That sound about right?"

Two were cut, and as the sun slid down the sky, and the Children of the Known dozed in their tents or peeked furtively through cracks to catch a glimpse of the Boatman, Summer and Orin wrestled the cross pieces into place and lashed them onto two of the longer logs to make a crude rectangle.

"Name all the kids who were in your class last year..."

"Tell me the names of any and all pets you've ever owned..."

"Well, that should be it," said Summer. "That looks like a raft to me. What do you think?"

"I say let's enter it in the Annual Bulkley River Raft Race!" laughed Orin.

"So, who's going to be the first to try it?"

"It was your idea," said Orin graciously. "You go first. Besides, if it's going to sink, I would rather it sunk with *you* on it!"

"It's not going to sink!" said Summer. "It's a wonderful raft."

The raft rocked as she pushed herself up out of the water and flopped onto the deck.

"See!" She stood up shakily, and the raft pitched violently from side to side.

"Hold onto it!" she cried.

Orin braced the swaying platform of logs.

"That's better," laughed Summer.

"Well, I hope you don't think I'm going to walk the whole way home holding onto the raft so you won't tip off!"

"It won't tip so much if we sit. Come on, try it."

The raft pitched again, and Summer screamed, but Orin managed to slide on his belly without actually knocking her into the water. When he sat up, though, the surface of the little raft was submerged by a good ten centimetres.

"It's going to be a wet ride," said Orin grimly. "Especially when we get a bit of food and your pack and everything on."

"Well, we've been wet all day, and it hasn't hurt us," said Summer.

"I had pictured something a little more luxurious," said Orin. "A little cabin on the deck where I could sit and rest out of the sun while you steered..."

Summer gave him a shove, his arms windmilled crazily, and he tipped into the water.

"It works fine with one person," Summer commented calmly, as Orin sputtered to the surface. "Maybe I should go on my own and send back the yacht for you."

Orin shook a soggy strand of hair out of his face and looked at her with squinting eyes. Summer expected him to lunge at any moment. But instead, he wiped his hand across his face and said, "Seriously, Summer. If we're going to go out on the river on that sinky thing, we might as well swim the whole way."

"You're right," said Summer, as she slid back into the water. "We need some bigger pieces of log."

Fifty metres upstream from their little lagoon, amongst the white trunks of the birch, there rose a single towering pine.

"We could cut it down, and it would land right in the water. We could float it down here."

"What if it just gets caught in the current and floats away?" cautioned Orin.

"I think it would float right down against the gravel bar," said Summer. "All we'd have to do is push it around to this side."

"Okay," said Orin. "Let's try it."

"Let's do it tomorrow," suggested Summer. "It will be dark soon, and I'm pretty tired."

"Are you making supper?" asked Orin.

"Sure," said Summer. "If you do the dishes."

"Okay, it's a deal. Let's knock off for the day."

They pulled the raft up as far as they could onto the gravel bar and made their way wearily back to their makeshift camp in a small clearing on the bench of land above the river.

Cooking supper consisted of opening an oiled packet of dried fish, and cutting a large turnip in two.

The two friends ate quietly. Both were too exhausted from the day's work to do anything else. When Summer had finished the last of the fish, she curled up with her knees under her chin and her head resting on her pack.

"Time to do the dishes," said Orin. He stood and picked up the knife. He wiped the blade on his pants, closed it and laid it beside Summer.

"Thanks," she said sleepily. The last thing she remembered was Orin's dark shadow standing there.

CHAPTER TEN...where their secret is discovered and Summer and Orin are taken to the Forgetting Place

When she woke up in the watery light of dawn, Orin was still standing there, now a dark shape against the pearly gray of the sky. The last star of morning shone on his shoulder. Summer wondered why he had stayed there all night, and in that instant she realized that it wasn't Orin at all.

"Good morning, Summer," said Tagg. "I have been waiting for you to wake up."

Summer sat upright. She looked around, half expecting to see herself encircled by angry faces, hands reaching to grab her and drag her back to the village. Instead, she found Orin sleeping, propped against a log, and the red-headed boy watching her with a faint smile on his lips.

"I see that you have been building a boat," said Tagg, turning his eyes toward the river.

"What if we have," she said defensively. "You can't stop us! We're going home!"

"I don't want to stop you," replied Tagg. "Hana said that you didn't believe her, but the things she told you are the truth."

"About the river?"

"About the river, about how you must forget, and how when you do, you will be of the Known, and you will not die."

"Nott died!"

"Nott was broken. Even the mountains can be broken..."

"That's just words!" snapped Summer. "He's dead and you know it."

"You will come to understand, when you have been here long enough, that there is a difference," said Tagg.

"I'm not planning to stay long enough, and I don't want to understand anymore!"

"You cannot return to the Unknown with your raft. You cannot return there by any way that I know."

"How do you know!" challenged Summer. "Have you ever tried?"

"There is a story..." began the boy.

"I'm tired of your stories!" said Summer. "You told me that no one dies here. That was a lie. I think you are lying about the river too!"

"What are *you* doing here?" Orin was awake

and rubbing his eyes. "What about the Boatman?"

"Yes," Summer jumped in. "I thought you were supposed to stay in your house for three days."

"I *am* the Boatman," said Tagg.

Summer and Orin fell dumb at the words.

"As Keeper of the Thread it is my duty to give the broken child and his stories back to the River."

"So it was just a story, all that about the children trying to go back, about the Boatman ... None of it was true."

"It is a story, yes," said Tagg. "But that makes it no less true. Nott's stories and his body have been given to the River. That is all we know for sure. The rest is unknown to us. In that way the story is true. He has gone to the Unknown, for all that is not of the Known is Unknown. All stories are true if you know where the truth lies in them."

"I don't care about the stories," said Summer. "We are going to finish our raft, and we are going to go home!"

"You will do what you need to do," said Tagg. "But before you do more work, will you come with me, and let me show you something?"

Summer glanced at Orin.

"It won't take long," said Tagg. "I promise."

Orin shrugged.

"We will follow the River for a time, but then the trail climbs. You will see."

The trio walked in silence except for when Tagg stopped to comment on a plant that grew beside the path, or to point out a bird circling high above.

Neither Summer nor Orin was in a mood to chat, and, for the most part, answered his observations with monosyllables and grunts.

The trail left the river and climbed steeply upwards across the face of a treed slope. Once in a while they could see the silver glint of the river below them, but each time it was further away.

At one point, the trail passed for a hundred metres along the base of a crumbling wall of rock. A precipitous slope fell away below them to the river. Summer noticed that Orin, walking ahead of her, kept his eyes steadfastly to the ground and looked neither to left nor right. "This is where Nott fell," Tagg said. "A rock must have come loose from above."

Orin seemed to sway, as if buffeted by a high wind. There was no wind.

"Luckily, he came to rest against that boulder there, or we would never have found him. Two of the mothers had to climb down on ropes to bring him up."

Suddenly, Orin gave a low moan and sank slowly to the ground. His face was chalky, and sweat glistened on his forehead.

"Orin, what is it?"

"I can't go any further," said Orin. "You guys go ahead. I thought I could do it, but my knees are like jelly."

"I forgot, you don't like high places."

Tagg knelt beside him, and put his arm around him. "We will hold you," he said. "It is not much further. Stand up . . ."

Reluctantly, Orin forced himself to his feet.

"You hold onto my belt and Summer will hold onto you. Look at my back and think about . . . about anything . . . We will be past this part before you know it."

"I'll have to go back again."

"You will have to go half way back in any case," said Tagg. "Come now, and I will show you a way not to be afraid on the way back."

The little procession inched along the path past the slope.

"I'm okay now," said Orin. Small trees and bushes grew along the slope below them. "If I fell here, I could catch myself, but back there . . ."

At last, they found themselves near the edge of a raised plateau that jutted before them like the prow of a gigantic ship sailing into the blue sea of the sky.

"How much farther is it?" asked Summer.

"We are there," said Tagg. "Come!"

He hurried ahead, and Summer and Orin had to walk quickly to keep up with him. Then they were at the edge of the plateau.

"You might not want to come too close," Tagg said to Orin.

"I would feel a lot better if you guys didn't stand so close either," he said.

When Summer stepped to the edge, she saw the reason for Tagg's warning. The cliff dropped straight down from where they stood, seemingly forever, into a great boiling cauldron of mist. To the left and far below, a tremulous, silent cascade of water shimmered into the mist.

"The River," said Tagg.

"I'm not watching," Orin said behind them. "If you want to kill yourself, that's your business, but I'm not watching."

Summer and Tagg glanced back to see Orin turn and stare steadily in the other direction. Then they turned their eyes back to the terrible panorama below them.

"And there..." He pointed to the right where a second tiny torrent trickled into the gorge. "Another river. All the rivers, all the waters go back to the mountain."

"There must be one big river at the bottom," said Summer. "The water has to go somewhere."

"Where?" said Tagg.

"I don't know," said Summer softly.

"You see then that the River will take you into the Unknown—into what is not Known. But will it take you where you want to go? Will it take you back to your mother?"

Summer stood looking down into the formless mist, her thoughts drifting, and swirling. For a brief second, she imagined herself swirling downward through the mist, twisting, tumbling, falling. And then Tagg's voice grabbed her and pulled her back.

"I will take you back to your raft now. If you want to go."

Summer turned away from the abyss.

"You must be hungry," said Tagg. "We will eat before we start back. Wait here."

He started back along the path, then turned off to the left and disappeared.

"Where is he going?" asked Orin.

Summer shrugged, but she thought she had an idea where the boy had gone.

"What can you see down there?" Orin asked.

"It's a deep gorge," Summer told him. "There's a waterfall where the river empties into the gorge, but it's all misty. You can't see the bottom."

"So Tagg was telling the truth. We can't go that way."

"I guess so," Summer admitted reluctantly.

"We're stuck here for good," said Orin. "What now?"

"I guess we will go for our Forgetting Times," said Summer.

"What if we don't want to?" said Orin.

"I don't know," said Summer. "Maybe it will be like Tagg says—a time will come when we will welcome the chance to forget. I mean, if you missed your dad bad enough, and you knew you were never going to see him again, it might seem like a good idea to just forget completely... I don't know. Here's Tagg."

The Keeper of the Thread came striding toward them with a bundle in his arms. He greeted them cheerfully and began to unpack a picnic from the bundle—dried and smoked fish, dried meat, flat bread, roots and berries.

"Where did you get all this food?" asked Orin.

"This is the Forgetting Place, isn't it?" said Summer.

Tagg smiled at her.

"Yes," he said, "this is the Forgetting Place. There is a shelter near the edge of the bluff, well stocked with food and water. I shouldn't have brought you here, you know."

"But it won't matter soon, will it?" said Summer. "Because we will come here for our Forgetting Times. We'll forget that you did bring us here today. All that we will remember of the Forgetting Place is what we will be told in stories..."

Tagg turned to Orin.

"You were frightened, Orin, where the path crossed the high slope above the river. When you have passed your Forgetting Time, you will have forgotten to be afraid of things that need not frighten you."

"Are you suggesting that I stay up here?" asked Orin. "By myself?"

"Every second day, I will come and call to you by the name you use now. When you do not know to whom I call, it will be time to give you a new name, and you will start a new life as a Child of the Known."

"Well, I don't know," Orin picked his bread apart with nervous fingers. "Summer, what do you think? We can't get back, right? We were just talking about that. Maybe it does make more sense to just do it and get it over with."

"You make it sound painful," said Tagg. "It isn't painful at all, I assure you."

"I can't tell you what to do," said Summer. "But once you've forgotten who you are and where you came from, there is no hope of getting back. None!"

"Is there any hope now?" asked Orin.

They ate in silence for a while. Despite the fact

that they had not eaten since the night before, both Summer and Orin picked at the food.

"I must return to the village by dusk," said Tagg, looking up at the sun. "It is the third day. I must be there when the villagers come out to celebrate the departure of the Boatman. Are you coming back with me or staying, Orin?"

He stood up and started to bundle up the food.

"I don't know," said Orin.

"Why don't you stay," said Tagg. "I will show you where the shelter is. If, when I return in two days, you wish to come back with me, you may."

"You promise to come back in two days?" said Orin. "How much will I forget in two days?"

"I promise," said Tagg. "You will forget only as much as you want to forget."

"Maybe I will stay," Orin said to Summer. "Just to kind of see what it's like . . ."

"It's up to you," said Summer wearily, and she turned and started along the path that would lead her back to the river, back to the raft, back to the village.

"I'll see you in a couple of days," Orin called.

Summer turned and looked at her friend. There were tears in her eyes.

"No," she said sadly. "I don't think I will see Orin Webb again ever. I hope we can be friends, whoever we are. Good-bye, Orin."

Then she turned and strode quickly away across the meadow.

**CHAPTER ELEVEN...in which the first story be-
comes the last story**

"Are you going to finish your raft?"

They had just passed the point where the path
crossed under the wall of crumbled rock.

Summer looked back over her shoulder. She
thought about how, the next time that Orin walked
along the path, he wouldn't be Orin at all. He certainly wouldn't be the friend that couldn't go anywhere without his music.

"I don't know," she said. "Maybe."

"If you decide to go—wherever it is the River
will take you," said Tagg, "I will miss you."

Summer was surprised.

"If you're going to miss me so much," she said,
"why are you so eager for me and everyone else to
forget who I am?"

"It is not for me to choose. It is the way it must

be. If you do not forget, you will long for your mother. You will suffer."

"That's not the real reason, is it," said Summer. "The real reason is that you are afraid of the Unknown. You are afraid that if I remember who I am and where I came from, and if I tell others about it, they might want to leave here."

"To leave the Known is to die," said Tagg. "All the Children know that. No one would want to leave."

"The Children do die!" protested Summer. She could feel her anger rising, hot along her neck. "Your Forgetting Time—that's the same as dying! I will never see Orin again, not the Orin I know! That's just as bad as when Larry died!"

"Orin may choose not to stay, and even if he does..."

"You know he will stay!"

"But when you have gone for your Forgetting Time..."

"I won't!" yelled Summer. She turned and ran down the path.

She didn't stop until she reached the makeshift camp by the river. She picked up the saw and went crashing through the underbrush toward the solitary pine tree that she and Orin had spotted the day before.

She attacked the tree furiously, dragging the saw back and forth with savage strokes, muttering through clenched teeth when the blade bound in the cut.

She slammed her knuckles against the rough bark, and they bled. Sweat ran into her eyes and mingled with her tears. It trickled down her spine. Her mouth was terribly dry.

Then the blade stuck tight.

"You stupid piece of junk!" Summer screamed.

She pulled and twisted, and the blade snapped. Summer stared at the broken blade dumfounded. Her anger seeped out of her—she was simply too tired to hold onto it any longer.

She leaned against the tree and rested her head on her knees. She shut her eyes and watched the swirling patterns behind her eyelids, willing herself not to think.

She had no idea how long she had been there, when she heard a twig snap nearby. She opened her eyes and lifted her head.

Tagg was standing in front of her. In his hands was the axe that Summer and Orin had taken from the tool cache. Without speaking, he stepped forward and rested the axe against the tree beside her. Then he turned and walked away into the forest.

Summer opened her mouth to speak, but the boy was gone. After a minute or so, she stood up and hefted the axe. She took a deep breath and swung it back. On the down-swing the axe bit into the trunk with a satisfying chunk. Summer twisted the head free and a large slab of wood fell away. She swung the axe back again.

Finally, the tree started to heel over. The high top swished through the air and smacked into the water. The current tugged at the tree and slowly coaxed it away from the bank.

Summer sat with her legs dangling over the bank watching the tree bob downstream. She watched it turn end over end in the current, until it was heading down the river butt first. She watched the butt nuzzle up to the end of the gravel bar. She saw how the top seemed to teeter first toward the shore and then away toward the middle of the river, and how, finally, it fell away. The tree tipped out into the current, and floated slowly out of sight.

Summer was surprised at how little she cared that she had lost the tree. A great, leaden greyness seemed to have settled on her. She settled back on the grass and closed her eyes.

When she opened them again, she felt incredibly heavy, as if a huge weight was pressing down on her. She sat up and tried to shrug off the heaviness.

The forest itself seemed to be smothered by the same sense of weight. Nothing stirred. The only sound was the relentless gurgling of the water. Even the sky was heavy, a featureless blanket of grey. The sun wobbled there like a gigantic orange balloon full of molten lead.

Summer looked around her, fascinated. The whole world was new and strange. Everything was tinged with orange from that weird balloon in the sky—the grass, the water, the trees, her skin, everything. The air was like thin orange syrup flowing around her, sticky and warm.

And there were butterflies, thousands of butterflies drifting on silent wings. No, not butterflies . . .

"Ashes!" Now she could smell the smoke and see it billowing black against the grey.

"It's a forest fire," she thought.

She jumped to her feet, knowing with every nerve in her body that she had to run. But panic seized her, and she found herself turning first this way, then that, her thoughts screeching at her like a room full of frightened monkeys:

"The village, warn them!"

"Get away! Run!"

"Orin, warn Orin!"

"Tagg will warn the village!"

"What if he didn't go back there?"

"Run!"

"What if they are still inside their houses and haven't seen the smoke!"

"Run!"

"Warn Orin!"

A hot wind scraped through the trees. The edges of the balloon began to dissolve until there was nothing left but a faint orange bruise against the deepening grey.

Summer saw gaudy orange birds leaping from tree top to tree top, and she knew then that she had no choice. It was too late to warn the Children.

She thrashed through the underbrush back toward the trail. As she burst onto the trail and started running, she remembered Larry talking about how fast a forest fire could move, and she wondered if she could outrun it.

"I have to outrun it!" she said to herself. "I have to get to Orin!"

As she slogged up the steep path toward the plateau, fire spread inside her too, until her legs and her lungs, her whole body, crackled with pain.

She gulped down air to try and cool the fire, and sucked in smoke instead. She began to cough so violently that she was forced to stop running, and concentrate just on getting breath into her lungs.

She stumbled on again.

The smoke seared her eyes until she was forced to close them. The coolness behind her eyelids felt delicious. Then her foot missed the edge of the narrow path, and she fell. She flipped and flipped again. Her fingers closed around the slender branches of a small bush. Thorns bit into her hand, but she held on until the bush's shallow roots pulled loose from the soil, and she began to slide. But the bush had slowed her fall; she was able to grab hold of the stem of a small sapling and stop herself. She looked down. The river tumbled far below at the bottom of the sparsely treed slope.

Summer felt for a foothold and began to climb. The path was three or four metres above her. There were small bushes and rocks that she could use to pull herself up. "I can make it," she thought. "I can make it."

Twice her feet slid out from under her, and she felt herself slipping back toward the river. But both times she was able to stop herself. Finally, she was able to crawl back onto the path.

She looked down the path back toward the raft. She rubbed her eyes, but the bobbing apparition didn't go away.

"Orin!" she called. "Orin!"

The patch of colour melded with the grey and disappeared. Summer shook her head.

"I'm starting to see things that aren't there," she said to herself.

She stood up, and tried to brush the dirt and leaves off her shirt. She winced with pain. Some of the thorns were still embedded in her palm.

"Summer?"

Summer's heart leapt at the unexpected sound, and she spun around. Orin was standing there with a puzzled look on his face.

"Where did you come from?" he asked.

"Where did I come from?" said Summer. "Where did *you* come from?"

"I didn't stay. I thought about it and decided that you were right. I had to come across that high part of the trail, but I made it."

Suddenly, Summer threw her arms around the startled boy. After a moment, he awkwardly closed his arms around her and hugged her back.

Summer pulled away and smiled at her friend.

"We've got to get away," she said. "See?"

* * *

'Fire! Fire! Fire!' The word flickered through the village.

Raven sounded the alarm: 'Fire! Fire! Fire!'

Bear came to warn them that the flames were near. The air grew hotter and hotter, the sky filled with ash until the sun shimmered ghostly grey. The forest creatures fled in terror.

The mothers gathered the children around them and prepared to leave the village. They ran, but the Fire ran as fast, and faster. At last they came to the River, and stood with their backs to the cool tumbling water as the Fire closed its arms around them.

When the heat was almost too much to bear, one mother speaking for all the mothers, turned and said to the River: 'Take our children. Care for them and keep them as your own. Better that you should be their mother than they should be devoured by the merciless Fire.'

And so saying, they took the children and hurled them into the water. The River lifted the children up and bore them along past the raging Fire.

* * *

"We have to get back to our raft."

"I don't know if we can," Orin said.

"We have to try."

As they got closer to the camp, the smoke became almost intolerably thick; and then suddenly they were below the pall, and they could see the forest in front of them wavering in patterns of black and red. The heat beat on them, forcing the breath from their bodies.

"We'll never make it to the raft!" Orin rasped.

Summer grabbed his arm. "Look!" she said.

She was pointing toward the river, ten metres below.

"What?" he asked.

"The tree..."

A tree trunk had drifted with the current until it had fouled against two rocks that jutted out of the swiftly flowing water. It rested at right angles to the current, forming a dam over which the water slid like a silk curtain.

"If we can get it free of the rock, we can float down the river on that," said Summer.

"Float where?" asked Orin.

"Away from the fire!" Summer said insistently. She began to scramble down the bank. Orin followed.

"It won't take much to swing it around the rocks," she said. "See how it's moving already. It's barely hanging on!"

She waded into the torrent, and immediately felt herself sliding away. She lunged and managed to grab hold of the rough bark.

"Watch out!" she called to Orin. "The current's strong!"

She held onto the tree trunk with one arm, and held her other hand out to Orin. He plunged into the water, slipped sideways, and at the last possible second, grasped her hand. He slid under the water, but managed to find his footing again, and dragged himself up onto the first rock.

"We'll have to crawl along until we're on the

other side of the rock, and then we can swing the top around."

Summer pulled herself onto the upstream side of the tree. Now the current pressed them in against the log. They inched along until they were well past the second rock. The force of the river pushing them began to pull the top of the tree around, and in a minute, it pulled free on the rocks and went bobbing away with its two tattered passengers clinging to it.

* * *

The Fire, angry at having been robbed, threw tongues of flame across the water and into the forest on the other side. Soon the River was flowing through the very heart of the fire and its cool waters were starting to hiss and steam.

When it seemed that the children were to be boiled alive, the River reared up and flung itself against the face of a sheer rock wall...

* * *

"Summer, look out!" Summer saw the horror on Orin's face and twisted around. Ahead of them, a blank, vertical wall of rock rose out of the water. The water beat against it, falling back on itself in huge, angry waves, and then, accepting that the rock would not move, went hissing and boiling through a narrow chute on either side.

The tree was heading straight for the wall of rock, and all that Summer and Orin could do was hold on and hope. The top of the tree rammed into the wall. Summer saw it bend and shatter, and then she felt herself being wrenched away and tossed, arms and legs flailing, into the water.

Summer felt water go up her nose and twisted to get upright. She felt a moment of panic as something grabbed at her. A high sweet voice sang in her ears—"Mother! Mother!"—and she imagined silver ghost fingers clutching at her. She tugged, and the branch that had snagged on her shirt snapped. She bobbed to the surface.

A moment later, Orin burst from below, sputtering and flailing his arms.

"Jeez! I thought I was going to drown!" he gasped. "I could feel something grabbing at me..."

They paddled to the edge of the pond, squelched through the sodden ooze and flopped onto the bank.

"Hey, I thought you two were supposed to be getting water!" Aleisha was watching them from behind the roots of the fallen tamarack. "Karen and me are going to take Ralph for a walk. You guys want to come? Hey, brother, you shouldn't leave your Walkman sitting around like this. Somebody might steal it."

"My Walkman?" said Orin. "But I left my Walkman back at Tagg's house..."

"Whose house?" asked Aleisha.

Orin looked at his wrist where his hi-tech wonder of chrome and plastic winked back unbroken.

"Summer," he said. "Do you remember what time it was when I looked at my watch before?"

Summer shook her head.

"I remember. It was 10:26. Look."

He held out his arm so that she could see the digital read-out. The tiny black numbers read "10:26". As she watched the last digit switched from a six to a seven.

"It never happened..." said Orin.

"Yes, it did," said Summer. "Or if it didn't, it will..."

"What happened?" asked Aleisha. "Tell me!"

"Nothing," said Summer. "Come on. Karen's waiting."

"Hey, don't forget your thong thing!" said Aleisha.

"Just leave it there," said Summer. "I'll get it later."

CHAPTER TWELVE...in which there are two fare-wells and a story

The next time they came to the pond for water, the thong was gone.

"Nott took it," said Orin.

"Maybe," said Summer.

"Does that mean all the things that happened while we were there won't happen now?"

"I don't know," said Summer. "Maybe if we're not there it all happens differently. Nott doesn't fall, there is no fire..."

"If there is a fire, I hope they get away okay."

"The Children would have gone to the river, too," said Summer. "If the fire did happen, they would have gone to the river. They've all heard that story so many times; it would be the first thing they would think of."

"Do you think the River saved them," said Orin. "Maybe it took them back to their mothers."

"Who knows," said Summer. "Maybe it took them somewhere else, somewhere else safe. I like to think that Tagg is back with his mother, too. I liked him. But maybe that isn't what he would have wanted..."

"I guess we'll never know..."

"No, we'll never know for sure. But they're safe, I'm sure of that. The River would have protected them." She crouched down beside the pool and dabbled her hand in the water. "I can't remember what he looked like," said Summer. "Not really."

"Tagg?"

"Yeah. I mean, I know what he looked like, but I can't *see* him in my mind. I think maybe it works both ways—the forgetting."

"Maybe we should write it down, make a book about what happened."

"I couldn't," said Summer. "I tried to tell Karen about what happened, but I can't. The words don't make sense—only when I talk to you."

"You're right," said her friend. "The same thing happened to me when I tried to tell Aleisha and Dad about it."

"I wonder if we'll remember anything about all this by next summer?"

Orin shrugged. "Who knows?"

Summer and Orin were standing together by the pond. The holidays were almost over. Orin and Aleisha were leaving in a couple of days to return to Vancouver in time for school. In the days and weeks since they had taken that tumble into the water,

Summer and Orin had returned again and again to stand beside the haunted pool and talk.

"Is this too silly, Orin? I was thinking that the water in this pool might be part of the water that goes into the river—the Forgetting River. Does that make sense?"

"As much sense as any of it."

Summer picked up a pebble and tossed it into the pond.

"Hello!" she said. the ripples moved toward her as if in response to her call.

"If you are Tagg's River," she said, "tell him that we miss him, and we hope he's okay."

"Worth a try," said Orin.

*　*　*

"I miss him," said Summer.

Karen put down the spoon that she had been using to stir the spaghetti sauce on the stove. She wiped her hands on a tea towel and came and sat beside Summer at the kitchen table.

"I miss him too," she said. She put her arm around her daughter, and slowly turned over another page of the photo album that lay open on the table in front of them.

"That's such a silly picture," Summer laughed. "I remember that. Larry was trying to teach Ralph to pull a sled."

The door swung open, and Orin and Aleisha tromped into the room.

"Smells good in here!" said Orin. He put a big bag on the counter. "Doughnuts!" he declared. "And

125

balloons. And a new 'Restless Fingers' cassette! We can't have a farewell party without music. You know, I don't think people should wait until they have to leave before having farewell parties..."

"Supper will be a few minutes yet," said Karen. "I'll put the spaghetti on."

"What are you looking at?" asked Orin, sitting in Karen's seat.

"Pictures of Larry and Ralph," said Summer. "Would you like to see them?"

Aleisha slid into the seat on her other side.

"Why is Larry pulling Ralph on a sled?" she said. "And why has Ralph got that goofy grin on his face?"

"Didn't I ever tell you about that?" said Summer. "It's a good story..."